THE STRIDER AND THE REGULUS

THE STAR OF ATLANTIS SERIES
BOOK 1

TRICIA D. WAGNER

LYRIDAE BOOKS

PRAISE FOR TRICIA D. WAGNER

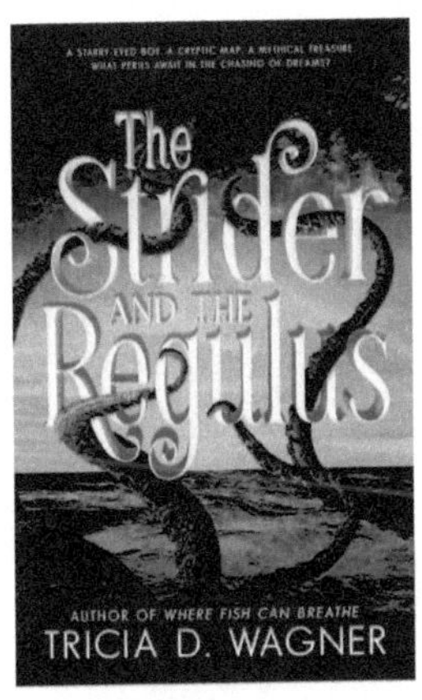

"A SENSITIVE AND ACTION-FILLED COMING-OF-AGE STORY, **THE STRIDER AND THE REGULUS** HAS THIRTEEN-YEAR-OLD SWIFT PROVING TO HIS FATHER AND HIMSELF THAT HE IS CAPABLE OF FAR MORE THAN EITHER OF THEM BELIEVED. THE STELLAR PROSE OF THIS STORY PUTS IT IN A CATEGORY OF ITS OWN AMONG YOUNG ADULT NOVELS."
-PUBLISHER'S WEEKLY BOOKLIFE PRIZE

"AS SWIFT LIVES UP TO HIS NAME AND HIS FAMILY LEGACY, YOUNG ADULTS RECEIVE A FAST-PACED FANTASY THAT WILL APPEAL NOT JUST ON THE ADVENTURE OR FANTASY LEVELS, BUT IN MATTERS OF THE HEART AS THE YOUNG STRUGGLE FOR INDEPENDENCE AND ACTION IN THE FACE OF PARENTAL RESTRICTIONS. TRICIA D. WAGNER'S ATTENTION TO PAIRING PSYCHOLOGICAL STRUGGLE WITH THE ADVENTURE OF FINDING A PROMISED TREASURE CREATES A STORY THAT PULLS ON THE EMOTIONS OF YOUNG READERS AS IT SATISFIES THEIR DESIRE FOR ACTION AND ADVENTURE."
-D. DONOVAN, SR. REVIEWER, MIDWEST BOOK REVIEW

READ THE STAR OF ATLANTIS SERIES!

The Strider and the Regulus, The Star of Atlantis & The Shepherd of the Stars

A starry-eyed boy.
A cryptic map. A mythical treasure.
What perils await in the chasing of dreams?

"Wagner has a beautiful and poetic writing style which serves to enhance the descriptive detail she provides to her novels. This gives her books a whimsical and otherworldly quality that supports the fantastical elements within them. Readers who appreciate thoughtful narratives that focus on the human condition within the context of charming and memorable stories will quickly fall for this series and its immersive quality.

"The medical and scientific elements found within this book help readers puzzle out the question of what is true in Swift's world alongside the legend and lore. This is a satisfying series that will speak to young adult readers and adults alike."
- Mary R. Lanni, MLIS, *Reedsy Discovery*

A ship is safe in harbor –
but that's not what ships are for.

\- John A. Shedd

1

*S*wift raced through the house, away from his father.

"I'm not finished talking to you," rang his father's voice—merry, but full of serious intent.

"Did you think trapping him would be so easy?" asked Caius, Swift's nearest brother, older by a decade.

Their father, Justus, chuckled. "Lad hardly gave me a chance to start."

Swift snuck out the back door, and with a smack of its metal on wood, silenced Justus and Caius.

He sprinted over the green and ducked into the woods, pounding the leaf litter toward a thicket crowded with old English oaks.

"Stay," Justus had pleaded. "Hear me."

But was he willing to hear Swift? Didn't seem he was. So why should Swift hear him?

Swift ran along a pathless course, dawn's misty light shafting through twisting boughs. Soggy leaves stuck to his ankles and shins, casting him in a skin made of woods, lending him a taint of moss and damp earth.

If only he could vanish so easily into these Devonshire woods as a part of them, sly and invisible as the fox whose path he was beating, whose musk was all that remained from its secret trek through the shire sometime in the night.

He slipped behind an ancient oak tree and clung to its broad trunk as to the coat of one trusted and ready to defend. Justus didn't seem to be following.

But Justus wouldn't give up so easily.

Justus seemed to believe he perfectly understood all his sons. And as he'd spoken the six most dire words—"It's time we had a talk"—he'd laid on Swift a gaze that seemed to blow him wide open, as a storm wind might part a glade to unmask a rabbit warren.

Those fearsome six words were the ozone-rich first breath of an encroaching summer storm.

The dreaded 'Justus Talk' was upon him.

A Justus Talk was the dulling of the sunset. The unsalvageable shattering of a ship.

A Justus Talk meant boyhood days were at an end.

All three Kingsley brothers who'd come before had failed to evade the Justus Talk, and so each had succumbed.

It was a Justus Talk that locked Trystan into clocking thousands of hours of cello practice while his friends grew up and moved away.

A Justus Talk propelled Edric into rugby, which yielded a short, amateur career that a back injury had finished.

It was a Justus Talk that had Caius reading medicine before his friends had even graduated.

But Swift wasn't anything like his brothers.

To them, he was nothing more than "the lad." Unformed and incompetent. Too wild. Too lost. Too childish. A bit young for even his own age.

And, as painful as it was to admit—they were right.

Even if Justus believed otherwise, as advanced as Swift was in school, thirteen was too young for anyone to face the threat of a Justus Talk. The others had been years older before having to deal with this.

Caius, though, seemed to think it was coming.

Swift didn't believe him—couldn't believe a Justus Talk could be anyplace close—

until last week.

Justus had initiated a friendly conversation with Swift, in the guise of pretending to want to see a pirate history book he was reading.

But Swift had smelled the rat and flitted away faster than Justus could blink.

He'd slipped along a creek in the woods that day, following a path to a muddy bank where it was unlikely Justus would follow.

And Justus hadn't followed.

One would think he might pick up the hint and give up the whole idea.

But today, Caius had been telling Swift about his medical school rounds, and all Swift had done was betray a sliver of interest and ask one meager question—shouldn't a specialist have been called in?

And Justus was on him, his eyes cobalt daggers, aiming to pin his final son and present a proof that he belonged on Caius' path—on his own path—to reading medicine.

"Who, at thirteen, could be expected to do such a thing?" Swift whispered to the oak.

The oak seemed to look down on him sympathetically.

"Well, not me," said Swift.

For as much born to medicine as Justus thought Swift was, Swift couldn't see it—much.

Rather, he knew—he just knew—that he belonged to the wilds. That he was meant for adventure.

Natural places like this—blowing woods and thrashing seas, windswept coasts and starry shores—seemed his perfect fit.

But this part of Swift, the greater part, Justus refused to see.

He'd probably already made up his mind to be disappointed if Swift didn't follow Caius. If he couldn't follow him.

"Swift," Justus called from the house. "I know you're close enough to hear me."

Cockle shards.

Swift flew deeper into the wilds.

These woods, backing up to Devon's north coast, were haunted with history, with the ghosts of the games Swift had played. Games of maritime wars and piracy and archaic people living off the land. Its sandy, bronzed earth offered countless good places to hide.

This grove had been planted by Justus' grandfather who, like Justus, like Caius, had been a doctor. But the stories Great Grandfather recorded in his journals—which Swift had read several times—made medicine sound more adventurous and less clinical than the anecdotes Justus and Caius told.

Justus insisted that Swift could improve on his "maturity" and "reserve"—that these weren't obstacles. He called Swift's interests—wonderful interests in things like sea adventures and stellar navigation and maritime myths and their legends of treasure—"the dregs of juvenility."

"Tell that to Great Grandfather, who served as a doctor on a Welsh ship," said Swift to the trees he sped by.

Great Grandfather, perhaps, was like Stevenson's doctor in *Treasure Island.*

If so, it seemed the track to medicine required less maturity and reserve, and more a good heart for adventure.

Swift crouched at the base of the broadest tree in the whole wood, whose limbs he knew like the rooms in his house.

"What does Justus know?" He picked up an acorn. "What will you be?" He shook it to hear its nut rattle. "A tree, of course. You're bound to be an oak tree."

Swift longed for such true understanding from the father he loved. If only Justus would take the trouble to really look inside Swift, his identity would show just as clearly.

"Swift?" echoed his father's voice—from the back patio, now.

Swift glanced around his blind. It was good enough for

the moment, well out of the sightline from the house and down a shallow hill. But it would be useless if Justus closed in.

He slipped further into the thicket.

It felt indeed childish, literally running away from his father. This certainly was at the level of a lad.

But Swift had to be firm on the point. Mum had confided in him that Caius and Trystan and Edric, all three, had all starkly changed once Justus got his claws in them.

Well, Caius less than the others, but over the last several years—since Caius has started medical school—even he seemed to have lost some of his joy.

"Maturity" and "reserve" and whatever other false skins Justus could bully Swift into might chase the life right out of him, pressing him into a mold that would cut out the truer parts.

Justus coughed as he did when he brought out his pipe. He was in the yard now, at least, if not moving into the trees.

Cockle shards.

Swift edged into a closely grown copse and crept along its narrow trail—a trail leading to a clearing behind the home of their closest neighbor.

There were some good hiding spots that way, but trying them would be risky. Ash, Swift's best friend—well, former best friend—lived there. Ash ventured outside as much as Swift did. Trekking too close to his yard would be chancy.

"I know these woods better than you do," called Justus.

Swift dropped to his stomach and stared through a crop of loose weeds.

A blur of motion told that Justus was standing at the edge of the woods, scanning the trees.

Swift slunk to the edge of their property, where boxwoods lined the clearing behind Ash's house.

He studied the clearing.

There was no one in Ash's yard. And these boxwoods were obscured pretty well from Ash's windows by a holly thicket.

Justus' footsteps crunched through the leaves.

Justus knew Swift avoided Ash. He wouldn't come looking this way.

Swift wedged himself into the green globes of bushes, their sharp branches scratching his hands and his cheeks. He ducked low until he could barely see above their crests.

Lifting just his eyes above them, he felt stealthy, as though he were a slick water monster, surmounting an agitated green sea.

"What in the world are you doing?"

Swift stood and spun.

There, right in the middle of the holly crop, holding a box of tackle and a fishing pole, stood Ash.

"You look a mess, all scratched up," said Ash. "Why are you in the middle of our bushes?"

"These aren't your bushes." Swift felt a fool to be caught— by Ash of all people—bunkering. "My mum planted them."

He tried to slip out of them gingerly, but there isn't really a graceful way to disembark from a bundle of bushes grown so tight that every move lays a mark.

"Yeah, she did plant those," said Ash. "On our side of the property line."

Justus' steps sounded closer.

Swift tripped his way out of the bushes.

"Aren't you wondering where I'm going?" Ash held up his tackle box.

Judging from the insulated wind jacket he wore, he must be headed for the Bristol Channel.

Cockle shards.

"My father and I are setting off to Lundy Island for some sailing practice," said Ash.

In the old days, whatever Ash was up to, he would've wanted Swift to come. Now, he mainly looked for chances to gloat.

"Then it's up the coast of Wales, around Pembrokeshire," said Ash. "All this rain will move out quick, Father says. We're in for some great sailing weather, for the rest of the weekend! It's going to be so much fun."

Swift narrowed his eyes. "Why the Welsh coast?"

Swift had once owned the greatest collection of Welsh sea faring books of anyone in the whole school.

Books of maritime histories and pirate tales and sea legends.

Now, though, almost his entire trove lay hidden—lay stolen—someplace inside Ash's house. Ash denied that he had the books, but he certainly did.

Ash narrowed his eyes right back. "I just want to look into something I read."

A crack rang in the forest—a twig breaking under a boot.

"I can't talk more," said Swift. "I have to scram."

"Why? What are you afraid of?" asked Ash.

Swift checked the forest behind him.

Justus was moving into the trees—casually, slowly. As though he put no stock in Swift's stealth or skill. Like catching him was no challenge. He was tending the wrong way, though.

Swift scanned the thicket for a better blind.

"Hey, there's your father," said Ash.

"Will you be quiet?" Swift whispered. "He's who I'm—"

"Mr. Kingsley," Ash shouted, waving. "You looking for Swift? He's right here."

Swift threw Ash a look. "Thanks a lot."

"Hey, it's my pleasure." Ash started back to his house, then turned. "I know your father hasn't taken you out on the water lately. You must miss it."

Though Justus loved being out on the water, he clearly loved his patients more. Several promises of sailing had lately gone stale.

"I don't need my father to go sailing," said Swift.

Ash cocked a brow.

And maybe he could go sailing all on his own. The Clovelly coast was within walking distance. Maybe Caius would loan him some money for a dinghy to rent, or for sailing lessons.

If Swift was old enough for a Justus Talk, he was old

enough to take on sailing. And if Ash could sail, then Swift certainly could.

"I'll bring you back a shell or something." Ash's large eyes harbored a growing satisfaction from the jealousy he must be reading on Swift's face.

Swift tried to conceal it, of course—he always tried to conceal his thoughts from Ash. But some feelings are like driftwood, liable to burble to the surface no matter what you do.

And the truth was—as cruel as Ash tended, he was adventurous and so creative. Swift had never laughed harder with anyone. He missed the old Ash.

But the old Ash was gone.

Swift cast him a sharp grin. "Lots of luck to you."

Ash, waving his rod, tossed back a satisfied smile. He trod through the holly thicket back toward his house.

What a numbskull. Ash might've appropriated Swift's love for the sea, but he'd left alone Swift's love for Old Norse mythology. He was oblivious that, in Old Norse, the words for "luck" and "hell" were the same.

Swift watched Ash until he was far gone, then muttered, "Son of a cock up."

"Let's watch that mouth, shall we?"

Swift spun.

Justus, biting his pipe.

Justus—completely relaxed, like a hunter who's bettered his kill and aims to toy with it before sending the blade home.

"Shall we speak?" asked Justus.

"Do I have a choice?"

Justus grinned around his pipe. "No."

Swift drifted down onto a boulder.

"Well?" Justus settled his foot on a thick stump. "What are your thoughts on one day venturing into medicine?"

The question seemed hypothetical enough to be harmless.

But—Justus wasn't wanting Swift to agree to "one day venture into medicine." He envisioned Swift gaining a competitive seat in a medical Practicum program for youth; graduating at the pinnacle of his class, and early; and ultimately topping his class at the university he himself had conquered.

This was Justus' one and only vision of Swift's future.

"Why get after me now?" asked Swift. "You didn't hunt Caius 'til he was fifteen."

"The Practicum program I'd like you to try for—for young lads aspiring to take on medicine—it didn't exist when Caius was your age."

Swift winked up into the strengthening sunlight. "And what if I told you that I'm just a young lad—not someone capable of taking on medicine?"

"Then, I'd say you don't know yourself."

Swift drew breath to argue, but—the way Justus was watching him—it was like he was measuring Swift and finding him exactly as expected.

Swift picked up an acorn and toyed with it. "I'd say I know myself."

Justus didn't ease up on the stare he was sending. He really believed he was right.

"That terrible morning"—Justus glanced at Ash's house— "when Ash tumbled into the water—your instinct was to save his life. Not everyone carries that reflex."

But it was that very tumble which Ash couldn't forgive. It was that terrible morning that'd ended their friendship. Though it'd happened five whole years ago, Ash would still tell anyone that his near-death accident was Swift's fault.

And the truth was—Swift hadn't saved Ash's life. Justus had.

"I'm no good with blood and such things." Swift lifted his bare, dirty foot, showcasing a scar on his heel from where a nail had punched in last winter—the ghost of the worst wound he'd ever suffered. "I went all black in the eyes and woozy when Caius pulled out that nail. Remember?"

"Dealing with injuries on oneself is far different than tending the bodies of others."

What part of—*what if I'm just a young lad*—could Justus not understand? Swift cracked the acorn in his fist.

"Lads your age can rarely see beyond their noses," said Justus. "That's where fathers come in handy. Will you not let me show you the Swift I can see?"

The Swift whom Justus saw was nothing more than some version of Justus himself.

Caius admitted that he could make out in Swift what Justus believed to see.

But Caius also said that, of all the brothers, Swift was the one most like Justus.

Caius was making the same mistake Justus always made— he was confusing similarity for sameness.

"After all, medicine runs in your blood." Justus looked about them. "This very grove was planted by your great grandfather—a renowned physician in his day."

Who knew but that Great Grandfather might've planted this grove out of some subconscious intuition that his some-day-great-grandson would need his solutions—places to hide when chased by a domineering father who overrated him.

From what Swift had read of Great Grandfather's notes, he seemed to be strongly interested in soothing not just illness and injury, but fear and pain.

And he never wrote of a case without critically adding what he could've done better—he called those parts, "healing the healer."

It was like he viewed the practice of medicine itself as a puzzle to work at. A craft to refine.

Caius and Justus rarely talked about medicine so plainly in terms of its capacity to evolve. And they talked more of processes and standards than they did about the simple ambition of easing the problem of pain.

"Imagine," said Justus, "what he might think of having a great grandson such as you—reaching the heights that you very well might."

If Justus thought Swift was capable of reaching the heights Great Grandfather aspired to, then he certainly couldn't see Swift. Even thinking of trying to test into the Practicum—cool though it might be—made Swift feel even littler, even more incompetent, than he normally did.

Being "the lad," seemed to mean that he wasn't just younger than his brothers, lacking "maturity" and "reserve."

It cast him as a different sort of creature entirely.

"I don't want to talk about this anymore."

Justus captured his glance. "Don't you, though?"

Swift eyed the thicket behind Justus.

Great Grandfather's grove was divided from a vast woodland by a measly fence.

He could run. He could jump the fence and run and keep running.

Justus could follow him, sure. But Swift could wear him out.

Justus, as though sensing the flight on him, moved in. "There's no future in scampering about, lost to wild games. You must choose a sound path. And selecting one sooner, rather than later, would be to your advantage."

Swift rested his hand on his pocket. "I already have a sound path."

Justus lifted a brow.

Swift's trouser pocket, without fail, contained a wonderful, old book: *The Star of Atlantis.*

It was the lore of a fabled lost treasure, hidden hundreds of years ago somewhere along the Welsh coast.

This book of sea legends—the best one Swift ever had found—also held the dignified office of being the sole remnant of his collection all but obliterated by Ash.

Justus tuned his eyes to Swift's pocket. "Let's have a look at that, shall we?"

Swift hesitated.

Justus held out his hand.

"All right, have a look." Swift drew out the book. "Tell me if it's even possible to hold that book and imagine a path more exciting."

Justus took it, focusing for a moment on the seven-pointed Celtic star on its cover.

"That star represents what the ancient Celts defined as elemental," said Swift. "The moon, wind, enchantment, the sea, spirit, Earth's forests, its sun."

These felt elemental to Swift himself, too.

Justus opened the book.

He studied, as he flipped pages, its hand-inked drawings of coasts and its actual old notes on navigation and weather; its sea shanties and poems; its sketches of mythical sea monsters haunting inked waters; its cryptic strokes, lining the top of each page, looking almost like the letters of some ancient, lost language.

His eyes, as he turned pages, widened.

That expression on Justus was the same as what he wore when he used to pretend with Swift. With his face so bright like that, he looked like Caius.

"How can anything—even medicine—compare?" asked Swift. "Those stories are thought to be true, about treasure hidden along the Welsh coast. And no one's ever found the Star of Atlantis."

Justus lowered to a knee before Swift. "Have I ever told you that I had a book similar to this when I was a lad?"

"About lost treasure? About the Star of Atlantis?"

"That's right," said Justus. "I, too, looked to the very same legends that have you so entranced."

"Where's the book now? Do you still have it?"

"Probably not," said Justus. "These things, you see...they do fade."

Thunder rumbled from the edge of a low storm.

Justus handed him back *The Star of Atlantis*. "The path I can set you on is quite as full of adventure and reward as what lies there. And it's steadier. You'll need a sound pathway, and soon. University, for you, is just a few short years away. Will you not lean where I'd have you go?"

It wasn't that the thought of leaning toward medicine wasn't intriguing. It truly was.

The stories that Caius and Justus came home with—Swift had to admit—were mesmerizing.

The idea of all the work it would be, trying to test into the Practicum—though it did seem daunting, even that wasn't too off-putting.

The truth was—medicine was riddled with suffering.

And death.

More than anything, it was that bitterness that seemed to magnify the incompetence Swift felt. He couldn't bear those dark places that Justus and Caius seemed to handle so effortlessly.

If Justus forced him into medicine, Swift would end up disappointing him. And Caius.

Swift backed away, toward a darkening, tangly stretch of woods.

If he ran now, Justus might feel he'd said plenty and decide not to follow.

"Come. The sky's bent on storming," said Justus. "Shall we go explore a legitimate pursuit?"

A large raindrop splashed on Swift's cheek.

"Quickly now," said Justus. "Before we're soaked."

"You don't understand," said Swift. "Treasure hunting, sea histories, sailing adventures—everything the star on my book represents—these are legitimate, too."

"It's not that you can't cultivate an interest in sea legends," said Justus. "Think of my dear friend, Elias, so brilliant a psychiatrist—he loves to be out on the sea. And I quite hold him responsible for teaching you to love its wonders and myths. Many doctors, like Elias, harbor quaint hobbies."

Quaint hobbies.

Justus watched Swift, one brow raised, as though he were reading plain text on Swift's face. "Edric and Trystan will have arrived from the station by now. Let's move this discussion inside."

What was it to Swift if Trystan and Edric had come home for the weekend? They were here to see Justus and Mum and

Caius—the only big brother left in Clovelly. They wouldn't care a bit whether Swift came in or didn't.

Swift glanced at Ash's house. "You keep telling me you'll take me sailing. You say you'll teach me all about it."

The sky let down more drops.

They were coming in slow, stuttering bursts, but they were big. This would soon be a hard downpour.

Good.

Justus studied Ash's house. "Is that what all this resistance is about? Are you jealous of Ash?"

Jealous?

Jealousy was exactly what Ash wanted from Swift. How could Justus even say that?

"I'm not jealous of anyone." Raising his voice never helped his case, but he couldn't help it.

Justus glanced back at their house. "Perhaps you'd value what your brothers have to say about the Practicum."

His brothers would no doubt join Justus in his campaign.

Edric, out of all of them, might best understand Swift's predicament. Edric wasn't anything close to straight-laced.

It was actually he who, at two years old, latched onto their father's first name and refused to call him anything besides Justus. Mum and Justus alike found it so endearing, they never corrected him.

And so by Edric's declaration, what'd once been a father was born as a Justus, and he was Justus to his boys ever since.

They all considered it an act of foresight on Edric's part, rather than a mere child's blunder. Their father was alike to a Thor or an Odin, deific and timeless. And to them, he seemed larger than life, aiming—with god-like determination—to raise them not just to manhood, but to magnificence.

In the end, though, Edric abandoned Justus' lofty aspirations to make a star athlete of him—and not just because of the injury.

As insightful as Justus was with his sons, Edric dared to claim to know himself better, and he forged his own way.

Now Edric was free as a kite, spending his time however he liked and running his own microbrewery.

But Edric had always enjoyed seeing Swift suffer. If Justus brought Edric into this, he'd only make everything worse.

Trystan always said he wouldn't trade Justus' guidance for anything, so he'd be no help. And Caius, though he seemed to care for Swift more than the others did, would say, just like always, that in Swift he saw Justus.

"Even if they agree with you, it doesn't mean I could follow you," said Swift. "To everyone, I'm nothing more than a lad."

"You're fluency with languages, Swift. You're the only lad I know who can speak eight of them—and you study more languages, yet—and not just the classical ones, but archaic. And, if we were to talk academics, your love of medical topics aside—your adeptness with science and maths—you've excelled beyond everyone in your entire school, not to mention the reach of your brothers."

"Being good at school isn't the point," said Swift. "In no way am I anything like my brothers."

"Perhaps, today, you can't see your potential in medicine," said Justus. "But I wager—you will. Why don't you come inside and ask them for yourself? My bet is that they'll say so, too."

"Caius calls treasure hunting 'great sport,'" said Swift. "Though I doubt he'd admit that to you. Trystan always agrees with whatever you say. And Edric would just tell me to get lost."

"That's not fair, not to any of them." Justus folded his arms tightly, a sure signal that he was losing his cool. "The plan has always been for you to start with a University at sixteen. Any way you look at it, we're close to that mark. And let me stress, Caius thinks my plan for you is splendid. He's a bit envious, actually, of your chance to compete to get into a medical Practicum, so young."

"That's easy talk for him," said Swift. "Caius didn't have

to deal with the threat of all this work, all this gore, at thirteen."

The wind drove in a sheet of rain.

"We'll not stand out in this downspout bickering like children on a subject so vital." Rain coursed off Justus' short beard. "I need you to hear me. It's time we take a hard look at this Practicum."

Swift already knew all about the Practicum—he'd stolen a look at the application on Justus' desk.

If Swift bought in, he'd be taking on a schedule that would smother out every inch of free time. He'd have no hope of cultivating 'quaint hobbies' of any kind, much less of finding time to explore what he liked and discover for himself whether medicine was what he wanted.

"It's a smashing Practicum." Justus relaxed his arms in what seemed like a last-ditch appeal for Swift to cooperate. To concede. "Once you consider all it includes, I fancy you'll be quite entranced." His mouth curled in a hopeful smile. "Perhaps you'll grow as spellbound with it as you are with that trifle of a book."

The storm broke. Water fell in sheets, drenching them.

Swift laid his hand on his pocket, keeping safe there *The Star of Atlantis*—a symbol, a guide, maybe—to the only venture he could see himself in; the venture that might be his if his father could just understand him.

"Lad," said Justus, letting the water strike and roll off him. "It's time we move forward."

Swift launched into a sprint through the dark, pathless woods.

2

Swift scaled his treehouse ladder, a sequence of wooden bars Caius had long ago nailed to the trunk of the gnarliest oak in their woods.

He heaved himself onto its rough balcony. From it, he watched Justus rush through the rain and hustle into the house.

Justus looked frustrated, and he probably was. His strategy to make Swift hear the Justus Talk had tanked.

He might come back. This treehouse was no hiding spot—Justus certainly had seen Swift climb. And anyway, it was the first place his family ever looked for him.

But Swift had made his point—how could a lad do anything but fail miserably at the plan Justus had conjured? Justus might leave him alone. For a while, at least.

The rain lightened, and the clouds lifted some, turning the storm into a sun shower.

Swift backed out of the brightness. He closed the treehouse door and settled on the floor. He pulled near a stack of books—library books on maritime history.

They weren't very good books. They were poor substitutes for what Ash had stolen.

But they still felt important and knowledge bearing, musty as they were, damp-feeling with age.

He shuffled the stack into a sprawl around him and rummaged through.

Here lay books on using stars for navigation; on mythical sea creatures and pirate legends; on ancient languages, some spoken by Icelandic pirates who long ago ventured to Welsh waters in their dashing Norse vessels; on the treachery of the North Atlantic and all the ancient ships she'd wrecked.

A couple of books were medical ones on anatomy that included Michelangelo and Da Vinci plates.

Those were ghastly and disturbing. But eye-catching.

It'd felt right to include them in the haul. He mainly got them to show Caius.

In the distance, a creak sounded from the house—the backdoor swinging.

A clatter of cookery in sinks and on stoves rang, and over its clamor peeled his brothers' strong laughter.

No doubt they were laughing at him. And no doubt Edric was leading the fray.

Swift shifted to his treehouse window.

"Swift?" Mum was leaning out the backdoor. "Your brothers are asking for you."

Early this morning, Mum had counseled Swift that he'd fare better with Edric if he could "show some maturity and reserve."

Caius, though, had caught Swift's eye and winked.

Caius never expected anything close to maturity and reserve from Swift. Caius was reasonable. He accepted Swift's wild play—he even liked it.

Edric and Trystan, though, didn't.

Well, Trystan might. He liked to play. Sometimes.

But Edric was like Justus—big in the shoulders and furrow-browed, absorbed in more worldly things than sea faring guides or toads found in the forest or legendary treasure or super-gluing models or reading sea adventures very loudly because that was the best way to feel the people in them.

Edric was all moved out, on his own—a capable entrepreneur.

And, at twenty-eight, even his hair was the scary salt-and-peppery silver of their father's. That hair seemed dignified, all by itself, warning off rogue little brothers.

The last time Edric had been home, Swift's play had gotten too rollicking for Edric's salty-peppery tolerance. Things ended in a bloody lip on Swift.

Edric apologized right after and said he hadn't meant to shove Swift so hard.

But how could he not have meant it? Caius had never shoved Swift.

Panicking over retribution, Swift told his parents it happened in a fall out of a tree.

It was believable.

But Edric still blustered out of the house before questions could be asked.

"Breakfast is ready," Mum shouted.

She'd spent the whole morning cooking a full English breakfast, starting with a crack-of-dawn trip to the farm.

It felt callous to reject that, to refuse to go inside.

But inside waited Justus.

And Edric.

"I'm not hungry," Swift shouted back.

She cast him a doubtful look.

She was sharp and had certainly put together that he was out here because he wanted to be alone; because he meant to avoid taking something head on.

"I'm staying out," Swift called. "I'm skipping breakfast."

Mum glared at him, the text of her expression plain: *grow up.*

But in his treehouse, all alone, surrounded by his books, growing up was way out of the question.

Swift broke his gaze away from the house with its critical mother and boisterous laughter and moved another stack of books near.

He sprawled onto his belly, knocking aside the medical

ones, and flipped through compendiums of Old-World sailing maps.

Beneath those lay biographies of Bartholomew Roberts and other actual Welsh pirates. Here, also, were two guides on tying sailing knots, and one holding diagrams of ships.

Just diagrams, though.

Skeletal images, bloodless. Windless.

Swift shoved the whole lot of them away and sat up. None of these held any real promise.

He drew from his pocket his own book—most heavy with promise.

It was a small book, compact enough to easily fit in a big jacket or cargo trouser pocket. It was blue gray like whale skin, and its pages were yellow like baleen.

The cover was soft as suede with age, and the seven-pointed Celtic star embossed there shone an untarnished silver.

And above it, in crackling, bright letters, scrolled words as good as any pathway: *The Star of Atlantis*.

The treehouse door flashed open.

Caius.

"You heard Mum calling you, yes?" he asked.

Swift shrugged. "I'm not hungry."

"You might've managed to shake Justus, but you and I both know you'll never shake Mum."

"I just need a minute to"—Swift glanced around—"straighten up."

Caius studied the mess of books.

"Looks like you stumbled on some interesting finds." His gaze landed on the brittle anatomy texts.

"Sure, if you like creep and gore." Swift kicked aside the one on wrecked ships. "If you don't mind that they're legend-less." He held up *The Star of Atlantis*. "This is the most interesting one."

Caius, climbing in, winced as though in pain. "Damn."

He shook his hand. Studied it.

"What's wrong?"

"Looks like we need to sand the balcony again." Caius held up his hand.

From the center of his palm jetted a thick splinter, a good half-inch long. "I'd hate for something like this to spear you."

Swift dropped his book and took Caius' hand. "Open your fist. Let me look."

He pulled Caius to the window and spread his palm beneath the light shafting in.

The splinter was deep. If its sharp tip moved at all, it might dig further in—that would be excruciating.

"Don't trouble yourself, all right?" asked Caius.

"Be still, let me look."

Even his handling it might shove the sliver in further.

But it was rough enough on one edge that he might catch it with a needle.

Then, the trick would be getting it out in one piece.

Which it looked like he could do—if he could widen the opening a touch.

That shouldn't hurt much.

"I have a needle or something in here someplace," said Swift. "Hang on."

Caius cradled his hand as Swift fished a first aid kit from under his bookshelf. He opened it and drew out a needle and set of tweezers.

"You sure you can do it?" asked Caius.

"I know, clean it first, and the instruments," said Swift.

"No, I mean—do you want to? I'm sure I could—"

A gentle parting of skin, a well-aimed grasp, an easy slip, and the splinter was out.

Swift ended by squirting on too much ointment and masking his blunder with a way-too-large bandage.

"Does it hurt?"

Caius admired the greasy dressing. "Far less than when the splinter was in."

Swift again picked up *The Star of Atlantis*.

Caius drew from Swift's book pile the text of Da Vinci

drawings. "Father's friend, Elias, gave me a book similar to this when I started reading medicine."

Swift glanced at its cover, showing a face with no skin. "And it didn't scare you off?"

Caius watched Swift sidelong, the way he did when trying to divine a brother's thoughts. "Should I look for it for you?"

"Don't try to trick me. I see what you're doing. I got that one mostly for you."

"Mostly?"

Swift scooted back a bit from Caius, maybe out of range of the probing.

The hint of smile on Caius was too delighted for so little. "I get it." Too knowing.

Swift turned away from the medical books, from Caius, so no interest could show.

Caius crawled to the door. "Shape up your things, then come and say hello to Edric and Trystan. If you don't, Mum will be the next one up. We both know you don't want that."

Swift watched Caius leave. The instant the door was shut, he was on his belly again, cradling his treasured book.

He peeled opened its fragile cover and turned yellow page after yellow page.

The Star of Atlantis was an old, old seafaring guide on navigating rocks rising like tentacles; on the monstrous tempers of whirlpools dashing reefs and ships alike, spilling gold into the water; on seafarers grappling with winds sweeping bone-white Welsh beaches and the wide and wondrous Celtic coast, and then beyond its shallows—pale as death—to the sapphiric North Atlantic.

No author was listed, but it was clearly written by a sailor.

Maybe a pirate—one who knew how to brave quasi-magical waters for sea-hidden treasure.

Swift traced the ragged pages.

Pages that the callused fingers of old seafarers once had touched, as those coarse men and ladies, tough as wooden beams, set off on sojourns through treacherous black waves, being mercenaries or corsair pirates, smuggling prisoners to freedom or questing for broad-shouldered, bearded kings, sailing declarations of war to tyrants.

The book opened with a verse, with even the melody scripted. The words and musical notes were handwritten, their ink—from an actual, old inkpot—blurred:

IN FIFTY YEARS *of sailing free –*
   I never thought my eyes would see
   the sun go red, the waves go warm –
   the clouds collide: the perfect storm.
   Yo Ho, Yo Ho – Crack the boom and bend the crow!
   Yo Ho, Yo Ho – Over the swell we go.

SHIVERS BRUSHED SWIFT'S BODY, from his back to his belly.

The shanty sounded just like he imagined a pirate song would. This book really must've been written by an actual, real-deal pirate. Must've been! He turned the yellowed page.

"Swift," Mum hollered. "Now."

Her voice put out all Swift's goosebumps.

"I'm done calling you."

She sounded more impatient that time, but her voice didn't yet carry that piqued *I'm coming for you* tone.

Swift widened his grinning eyes and ventured on:

THE MEN ALL DRUNK, *locked in the brig,*
   I drain the grog and stay the rig!
   The men asleep, the sea in rage,
   the kraken creeps from out its cage.
   Yo Ho, Yo Ho – Flair the jib and jet the bow!
   Yo Ho, Yo Ho – Into the waves we blow.

· · ·

THE YELLOW of the book made it look baked. Baked by sun and stars and moon, weakened by water and wind, and all the better for it.

With its lick of pirate verse, with its diagrams of blotchy ink, with its leather cover, the small book was savory.

Probably, it would even taste like salt. He tapped a corner of a page to his tongue. It did taste like salt.

He pushed to his knees and flipped a few pages to see beyond the pirate verse, to a layout lined with sketches of sea monsters.

The text inside the circling monsters read:

When the shore draws long and straight, skim the briny banks. Be swallowed by Sterncastle Cove. Seek the islet, round as Earth, studded with Kraken fangs. Mind the deeps for mermaid tails, shimmering blue and green. Heed their song, but touch the water not, lest your life be forfeit to their goddess. Always keep a weather eye on the mist coiling in the cove, for through it paddles old Grog Blossom, always dead, yet ever awake, cursed to forever sail as watchman over the Star of Atlantis.

Swift sat back, positively sparkling with goosebumps.

He flipped onto his back and fanned the pages, blowing himself with a chill wind—the dregs of storm clouds.

He readied himself to start in on the verse again and see if he could get more goosebumps going, when—

The back inlay tore away from the cover.

From it, an envelope slipped and dropped onto his nose.

Swift sat up.

That last page had been deftly glued to a hardened cover —so perfectly, he'd never suspected that something might lay hidden.

He peered out the treehouse window at Mum, staring at him through the kitchen curtains.

What would she say to this—an actual pirate secret? What would Justus say?

Swift picked up the envelope.

It was thick and just as yellowed as the pages.

Just as old.

It was unmarked.

Swift loosed its brittle flap.

Inside was tucked a large sheet of parchment, folded smaller than the book by an inch. He carefully drew it out.

The sight of ink bleeding through the paper swiped Swift's breath. The parchment had been penned by hand—ink from an old inkpot, too.

Swift unfolded the parchment until before him lay a map of a forest.

He knew this forest.

Two of its edges were scalloped, rendering it obviously as the Wentletrap Forest—an ancient, vast woodland in Pembrokeshire, stretching dozens of miles up the western Welsh coast and spreading deeply inland.

The Wentletrap was said to be a maze of broken trails and eerie paths winding to no place among its arthritic, great trees.

Hikers reported as lost in the Wentletrap often were found dead, just at its brink—as though they'd died of exposure just minutes from escape.

The map didn't seem to offer any insight as to its structure or trails, but its perimeter was outlined in intricate detail.

Odd pen marks were cast along the edges of the map, and more weird ink strokes lay within the drawing of the Wentletrap itself, in sort of a winding pattern.

This struck Swift as clever. A wentletrap, after all— scientifically speaking—is the interior whorl climbing, like a spiral staircase, to a seashell's pinnacle.

His family owned a beach house nestled just at the fringe of the Wentletrap, and though he'd never been allowed to wander within it, for how treacherous it was rumored to be, he'd always felt drawn to it with its ancient oak trees and profound stillness.

Standing at its edge felt as entrancing, as promising, as standing on the shore of an emerald sea.

Swift opened *The Star of Atlantis* and compared the

artistic pen strokes crossing the top of each page to the pen strokes he was finding on the map.

Though not completely identical, they looked similar—like runes from the same forgotten alphabet.

And on one corner of the map, the pen strokes lay in perfect rows, in distinct groups—like word lists or sets of numbers. This, more than anything, made them seem like a language.

Swift pulled close one of his ancient language books and flipped through.

He went section by section, comparing the marks in the book and on the map with each.

The marks weren't hieroglyphs. They had nothing in common with Ancient Egyptian. They seemed sort of cuneiform, the way some were drawn in clear wedges.

But not one of the characters closely matched any language he could speak, nor any of the dead and dying languages he studied. Not even any of the cuneiform ones—not Hurrian, not Phoenician, not Elamite nor Sumerian, not Celtic Akkadian.

Perhaps it was a language so old, or a dialect so rare, as to have been entirely lost.

Or maybe this wasn't any language at all—maybe it was nothing more than simple marks added for artistry.

Swift held the map in a beam of sun and studied it whole.

The Wentletrap drawing took up about two thirds of the page, and the rest was given to the rugged Welsh coast, running alongside the forest.

Though the map of the Wentletrap Forest seemed as confounding as the real thing, the map of the ocean was easy to read, all its features beautifully done and its notes plain.

The trails of winds and currents were marked so clearly, as were detailed coves—nestled among realistic, jagged anchorage rocks.

Waves were sketched here and there, and from them slipped tentacles and fins.

Swift flipped through *The Star of Atlantis* to the riddle-seeming description of the way to the treasure:

When the shore draws long and straight, skim the briny banks. Be swallowed by Sterncastle Cove.

And on the map—the shore was drawn long and straight.

"This has got to be Sterncastle Cove," said Swift.

In the center of the drawing of the sea, inside a cluster of jetting boulders, there lay a silver, seven-pointed star—a Celtic seven-pointed star.

Swift held the cover of his book beside it.

They perfectly matched.

And on the map, above the star's highest points scrolled tiny, clear words: *The Star of Atlantis.*

Here, then, he held—a treasure map.

This was the real deal.

Swift rested the map on the treehouse planks before him.

It was unlike any treasure map he'd seen in books before. All others were cartoonish—a badly-drawn hand pointing to a vague location.

This was a meticulous, practical map of navigation, ports, and coves. It reminded him of the scientific guides Justus studied in preparing for sailing.

"Justus," whispered Swift.

Justus was wise, tough, and strong. He was brilliant as Odin—the Chieftain, the Ever Booming.

Justus was the greatest sailor (to luck with Ash and his father) and could doubtlessly find his way to this place, even with its circling pools of currents and surfacing monsters.

A ribbon of text outlined the edges of the map, just outside the cryptic pen strokes.

Its starting point read, "Seafarer's Oath."

Following that:

Come hell. Come storm waters. Come the Kraken. I'll forsake all sound shores for the night-lighted passage-

*ways—untrodden reaches—for sun-brightened visions,
for insights of stars.*

The way the strange marks were drawn, just beneath the oath and following it—it was almost as though they echoed the oath as some kind of translation.

Swift held the map at arm's length and studied its coastline and waters.

He knew enough about nautical navigation to make basic sense of what seemed to be sailing notes.

He could actually go after this.

Closing his eyes delivered him the whole picture—

There he was, climbing the crow's nest, calling orders, while Justus sailed the ship. There was Caius, posted on lookout at the bow. There were Mum and Trystan in the galley, making Devon cream tea. There was Edric, in the brig.

If they chased this—if they actually discovered the Star of Atlantis treasure—Swift's path would be set. What could Justus say? No one could force him down a path that would clobber him.

Mum threw open the treehouse door.

Swift startled up.

"Breakfast is ready, and your brothers are anxious to see you," said Mum.

Swift exploded from among the books. "Look, Mum, look."

"It's very rude of you, bunkering like this, ignoring everyone."

He lifted the map so carefully and hurried it to her. "I found this hidden in my book. It's an old, old map—see?"

Mum barely glanced at it. "I certainly don't have time to play around just now."

"It's a guide to hidden treasure," said Swift. "A guide to the Star of Atlantis."

"I must tend the stove, and you must come pay respects to your brothers." She started to climb down, then turned again. "Now."

"Hang the stove," Swift pointed right at the map's star. "Pirate treasure—hidden riches—someplace off the coast of Wales! We could live like royalty if we went after this."

Mum took the map and set it aside. "Breakfast first. Then you can tell me all about it."

If he discovered the Star of Atlantis, there'd be no call for growing up. A Justus Talk would be needless.

And between Swift and Ash, Swift would have the very last word. Ash would be the one thornily jealous.

Swift gently folded the map and placed it in his book. He pocketed it and followed Mum down the ladder.

3

S wift slipped into the dining room where his brothers and father were seated.

It felt like his book was burning through his pocket; like his heart was burning in his chest. Standing in the doorway, knowing what he'd found, made Swift feel accomplished the way they all were.

He'd managed to discover a map to lost treasure despite how Justus dismissed his love for sea lore; despite how Ash had tried to strip him of it, book by book.

He felt no longer remiss to be part of their company but could imagine himself like a peer—worthy of their acceptance. Maybe their admiration.

And all this at just thirteen.

He didn't have to try for any medical Practicum to win their respect.

Wait 'till everyone heard.

Trystan, who worked at a farm that had orchards and berry groves, was showing Caius and Mum a bottle of blackberry cider. He only worked the farm between practices and performances with the symphony, but he took great pride in it. He looked very pleased as he pulled out and handed them more cider bottles and jars of berry jams.

Trystan met Swift's eyes and smiled genuinely.

Trystan was a gentle person and had always been tender-hearted.

Hopefully, he wouldn't feel outdone when Swift revealed the treasure map.

Edric and Justus, seated alongside, were immersed in conversation.

Seeing Justus and Edric together made them both seem all the more intimidating. Edric had been born back when Mum and Justus lived in North Lancashire, and the tone of Edric's voice even sounded like Justus. Swift, who'd spent all his life in the West Country, but for summers in London, didn't sound anything like them.

Swift waved at salty-peppery Edric. What would he think of this?

Edric tipped up his fingers and kept talking with Justus, in close confidence.

It seemed there was no chance Edric would care about the map. If there were any way to contort this happy moment into something menacing, Edric would find it.

Swift found he couldn't move a step closer.

The way Justus and Edric were both watching him as they discretely spoke, it felt like they were talking about him.

Swift had something wonderful, yes, but—would any of them appreciate it? Mum hadn't thought a thing of his discovery.

"Picked and pressed these blackberries myself." Trystan poured juice into Swift's glass. "Are you going to sit down?"

Swift took his place by Caius and whispered, just to him, "I found something pretty great today. Something, I promise, you've never seen before."

Caius' eyes lit.

"What's the lad gotten tangled in now?" asked Edric.

Swift focused on Caius. "Try to guess what it is."

Caius propped a foot on Swift's chair. "Let's see. I bet you found a snake."

"No, you've seen a snake. This is a one-of-a-kind kind of something. And it's not an animal."

"Did you find a girl?" Trystan leaned across Caius, his eyes brightening. "I've never seen you with a girl."

"Yuck, no." Swift sipped his juice. "Keep guessing."

"Any girl to catch the eye of the lad would have to be part animal." Edric reached to scruff Swift's head of corkscrew curls.

Swift ducked.

Edric's hands were tough enough to leave bruises, even when he was calm.

"I give up," said Caius. "What did you find?"

This was it.

This could change everything.

Swift set aside his juice. "I found a pirate's treasure map." He could hardly breathe for the pleasure of the words. "A real-deal, swear-to-god, yellowed, pirate's treasure map."

Justus, seeming absorbed in thought, kept at his beans and sausages.

"Yellowed?" Caius raised a brow. "Then, it must be old."

"Old as the sea." Swift stood and looked at each of them. "And marked with a star—the Star of Atlantis." He pulled out his book, swollen with its map. "I found the map hidden inside the cover of my book."

"May I look?" asked Trystan.

Swift handed him the map. "I know it's legit, because even the paper is dusted with salt."

"If the paper's dusted with salt," said Edric, "I'd guess it came from a peanut box."

Justus, half-smiling, glanced at Edric.

"You're way off," said Swift. "The book's antique. And the map's hand drawn. Open it."

Trystan unfolded the map. "A map of a forest. How interesting."

Caius leaned in. "The way it's scalloped on two sides— that looks like the Wentletrap Forest."

"Who would take the time to draw a map of a scary old

forest like the Wentletrap that nobody cares to ever go in?" asked Edric.

"You're not getting it," said Swift. "It isn't a map of a forest." He pointed at the drawing of the sea. "Look at the cove—that has to be Sterncastle Cove. And look at that island. And, on the island—a star." He stared at Justus. "It's a map to the Star of Atlantis."

Justus finally looked at him.

Edric took the map from Trystan and examined it. "Even if that's supposed to be some particular cove, this map wouldn't help anyone reach it. I mean—the Wentletrap Forest is massive, and the map certainly isn't to scale. This drawing of the water might be any one of a hundred fussy-tempered little coves edging Pembrokeshire."

Swift locked eyes with his father. "Maybe you could take me out to sea." He shook his antsy legs to wiggle out the thrill. "Maybe we could sail to find the Star of Atlantis."

"Best to leave old treasure maps alone," said Justus. "Aren't they likely to be cursed?"

Why would he not take this seriously? The map was right before his eyes.

"All the better," said Swift. "Will you take me?" The thrill was manifesting in hopping. He couldn't stop the hopping.

Edric dropped his gaze off Swift and focused on his plate.

Mum eyed Swift, telegraphing her singular message. *Grow up.*

Swift drew the map away from Edric and held it where everyone could look at it. He straightened, mimicking Edric's salty-peppery dignity. "Or we could all go."

The times of being all together were thinning, now that the pair of oldest brothers had left Devonshire. If Justus wouldn't pay mind to the map, he might at least realize the chance for memory making and get excited. Maybe.

"All together," said Swift.

Justus didn't seem to be listening.

Swift stepped closer to him. "Please?"

Edric glanced up. "Begging like a baby doesn't suit you."

Mum sent a tiny smile Swift's way. She seemed to realize he was trying.

She widened the blinds. "The storm is clearing, leaving us with quite a fine day." She glanced at Justus. "Perhaps you'd like an afternoon sailing? I'd enjoy a trip to the beach house."

"Of course you would," said Swift. "See? Mum thinks it's a great idea."

"Another time," said Justus. "I've patients to read up on."

Swift gazed at the map's smart landmarks, its brave oath, its frights, its cryptic markings.

But no one else was looking at it.

He settled back into his chair.

Many of the books Ash had stolen were just as old as *The Star of Atlantis*. Swift had scored them over years of tagging Mum through estate sales and dusty bookshops.

Some, he found bearded with cobwebs, like they'd been unearthed from an old forgotten cellar, kept secret by an actual sailor.

Or maybe donated when some old pirate's hideout had been ransacked, after the pirate had been goaded down the plank.

What if it was a common practice, stuffing treasure maps inside old books? Swift had never thought to examine any of their covers.

What if, inside Swift's stolen books, Ash had found maps too?

"If we don't go after the Star of Atlantis soon, it might be pillaged before we can reach it," said Swift.

Justus pointed his fork at the rubbish sack pile that'd accumulated by the back door.

"You, lad, haven't done your chores."

"Hang the chores. We're talking pirate treasure. Gold and galleons. Ancient riches. Jewels and fame!" Did they not get it? This would change all of their lives.

Justus went back to eating.

Swift tucked his hands beneath him so he couldn't prop his chin on them and give in to the sulk that was rising.

Because actually, Edric was right.

Begging didn't suit him.

It used to work, at times, but its magic had blown out in the last few years.

Lately, his parents had stopped responding to him on any score unless he presented "respectful discussion," "careful reasoning," and "sound rhetoric."

Behind Justus, on the wall, hung a portrait of his pride, his ship—his *Regulus Borealis*—his small French-classic brigantine.

The ship against its sky looked sharp. Its masts, full sailed, looked like ridges lining the spine of a key.

Swift brought out his hands and laid them on the table. He molded his face into its best casual expression—the one with the most maturity in it.

Sitting tall like this, even his corkscrewed hair felt a touch less wild. Maybe there was a bit of salt and pepper inside, working its way out.

He thought about the word *nonchalance* as he said, "Perhaps a treasure map is childish." He folded the map and fed it with the book into his pocket. "Yes. I was mostly only kidding about it. What I really hoped, Justus, is that you could show me something about sailing today. The others could come along if they wanted. Either way, I wouldn't really mind."

He focused on the beans on his plate and ate them fork-and-spoon, the way Justus was doing.

He tuned an ear to the Pachelbel cello strains streaming from Mum's player in the kitchen and sipped his cider, studying the glass like the others did when they held wine.

Justus captured Swift's gaze and held it.

Though Justus had bequeathed his salt and pepper and stolid brow to Edric, he'd given only Swift his eyes. The blue of them seemed sometimes cobalt, like a rolling sea at the height of sunlit summer. At other times, they seemed glacial, pale as an ice floe. The charcoal limbal rings rimming his irises set the blue off, like steely negatives of eclipsed suns, giving them a tincture of wildness.

Justus wasn't wild, though.

He was reason and perception.

Swift, caught in his gaze, felt seen. Known.

The clock in the corner chimed its solemn pronouncement of the half hour in its tedious mood.

The chime rang at precisely the best moment—at the moment when Swift's back was at its absolute straightest. When Justus was lending focused attention his way.

Swift held stone still, hardly breathing, waiting for the pressure of the assessment to let go of him.

"Would you really be game for a true sailing lesson?" asked Justus.

"Yes." Swift pulled the book out of his pocket. "Of course I would—yes."

"You sure about that?" asked Trystan. "You might like the idea of the *Regulus* well enough. But learning to sail a ship is quite a different matter than riding along. Even enthused as you are, you might find it overly complex and exhausting."

"I've done more than just ride along," said Swift.

Truth be told, though, Trystan was right. Swift had watched Justus and his brothers sail plenty—but he'd never really handled the canvas and ropes.

That wasn't his fault, though. They'd always elbowed him out of the way.

Justus, staring at him, seemed to be measuring him.

And for good reason. Depending on what temper the sea and sky were in, history was against Swift—he could very well wind up seasick or sunsick, wallowing in humiliation alone on the bench in a matter of hours after they set out.

"Your ship could use some engine oil," said Caius. "Some action."

Swift returned Caius' subtle smile. "I do want to learn to sail, truly."

The shimmer of the Celtic Sea, daunting as those waters were, always had felt like a call. And now that he had an actual map to waiting treasure—

Swift tightened his fingers around his book with its map.

He had to follow this to Sterncastle Cove. He had to seek the Star of Atlantis.

If Justus wouldn't teach him to sail—if he wouldn't take Swift to search for this treasure—Swift would find another way.

Justus' eyes, fixed on Swift's, seemed full of knowing.

Swift pulled his gaze away from his father and laid it instead on the portrait of the *Regulus*.

Justus glanced over his shoulder at the picture. "Well, then. Perhaps we'll take out not just the *Regulus*, but the dinghy as well."

Fireworks went off inside of Swift. He held his breath to corral them all inside.

"You sure he's ready to try his hand at the *Strider*?" asked Caius. "Setting him to work on the *Regulus* will be a tough enough lesson."

"Why not?" asked Justus. "You yourself piloted the dinghy solo at his age."

Swift kept his face drab and plain, though the expression behind the calm facade felt twisted in an impish grin.

He didn't say another word as he settled his book and map safely inside his pocket; as he finished his breakfast, very politely.

Finally, he dabbed his mouth. "Might I be excused?"
Mum nodded.

"Gather yourself a case of warm clothes," said Justus. "We may as well sail up the Pembrokeshire coast and camp. That way you can have some practice with several different winds."

Swift pushed back his chair and rose. "Thank you, Justus."

He strolled until he was out of anyone's sightline, then charged—bolted—raced—flew up the stairs, down the hall, and into his room.

This very morning, he'd be sailing underneath an open dome of sky, floating on a strong ship in a blue world holding waiting treasure.

No Justus Talk was required to get Swift where he

needed to go. No pathway to medical school was necessary to satisfy his father's ambitions.

The moment the *Regulus* left the dock, Swift would be well on his journey, trekking his very own pathway.

He was older, taller, and stronger than he'd ever been. Surely, he'd be able to handle the rock of the boat and the elements and the complexity of canvas and lines.

As soon as Justus started in, actually teaching him, he'd find that Swift could easily learn all there was to know about sailing.

As quickly as he picked up languages, medical terms, maths, biology, and chemistry, he'd learn to master the *Strider* and the *Regulus* alike.

And so very soon, he'd be the discoverer—the unlikely, brilliant, born to the sea, child discoverer—of an artifact seafarers, for centuries, had sought and failed to excise from the ocean: the mythical Star of Atlantis.

4

*J*ustus waited for the sound of scrambling boy feet to die away. He glanced at his wife, Adara. "This is going to be fun."

Edric set down his knife. "You're not seriously considering letting Swift work the *Regulus*. He's only thirteen. And a young thirteen, at that."

Justus glanced up from his plate.

"He's not so young."

"You let him on the *Regulus*, on the *Strider*, he'll be fixed on nothing but chasing that treasure," said Caius.

"That's fine," said Justus. "If fabled treasure corners him with me, so be it."

Trystan sat back, grinning.

"You really think the lad's capable of sailing?" asked Edric.

Justus wiped his mouth. "He's capable of more than you think. More than he thinks."

Edric folded his arms. "You'll be doing all the heavy lifting, with that lad buzzing about you like an insect, niggling you to sail him to his treasure."

"Father won't be doing the heavy lifting," said Trystan, still grinning.

Justus winked at him.

Trystan glanced at his brothers. "On the ship, Swift will have nowhere to run. Father's found his chance to pin him for the Justus Talk."

"Ah." Caius set down his fork.

Edric, chuckling, set away his beer. "Lad doesn't stand a chance."

Indeed, Swift didn't stand a chance. Confined on the *Regulus*, he'd have no choice but to listen. And maybe, he'd finally hear.

"I hope you lot will be supportive," said Adara, pinning each of her sons in her way. "Swift certainly is capable of what your father has in mind for him. I'd thank you to help him see it."

She focused on Edric.

"If you treat him as incapable, that's certainly how he'll see himself."

"The lad may have some capability brewing," said Edric. "Still, he's little for a Justus Talk."

"Father's been trying to pin him," said Caius. "Swift knows and keeps slinking away."

"He's got loads of growing up to do before he could hear you, much less respond," said Edric, "what with his pirates and sea monsters, his stars and his ancient languages."

"Perhaps," said Justus. "But I surmise that Swift merely lacks focus. If he's to reach his potential, he needs the shaping now, unwelcomed as it may be."

"Swift has focus enough," said Caius. "He just isn't centered on medicine, as you'd like him to be."

Justus glanced at each of his sons. "Care to contribute a couple of days to the cause?"

"He's slippery," said Trystan. "Even on your ship, you'll have quite a time pinning him."

"Trystan isn't wrong that Swift is clever," said Caius. "Not to mention, he'll be determined to get wherever that map leads."

"The lad's brilliant, no less than he is cunning," said Justus.

"Academically, he's simply a savant, reaching heights that none others in his school ever have. Especially in maths and in sciences, which is quite telling. And how well he absorbs and retains languages—does that not betray a great patience for difficult matters? It's time we tune that brilliance."

"It'll take more than brilliance for him to catch your wind," said Edric. "Lots of brilliant people never quite find their purpose."

"Every day, I see new hints of potential in the lad," said Justus. "Glimmers of his abilities—every bit as stark as gold glittering under the sea."

"Swift's head is full of legends and treasure—a boy's dreams," said Caius. "Would it not be best to simply leave him with those dreams?"

"He needs to recognize how rare, how valuable—what a treasure—is his mind," said Justus. "Veiled as it now is by the mists of such dreams."

"What exactly do you have in mind for him?" asked Trystan.

"The lad's got the raw material for medical school," said Justus.

"I could see that for him, someday," said Trystan. "But he's only thirteen."

"I mean to lead him into a new program for youth aspiring to read medicine," said Justus. "Applicants must be thirteen. If Swift manages to pass the entrance exams, he'll begin the Practicum at fourteen."

"He's not got the stomach for medicine," said Edric.

Justus waved off the doubt. "Constitution, he can build. There's no better course to set him on now, if he's to start in a University at sixteen. The Practicum would mean a guaranteed seat and strong scholarships. Anyway, he's mad about what Caius is doing. Our talking shop rouses his curiosity."

"But he doesn't brighten at medicine the way he does when he's lost in some guide on stellar navigation," said Caius, "on legendary voyages and ancient ships. He still is very much a boy."

"This is precisely the issue I aim to remedy," said Justus. "Swift doesn't yet know himself. He needs some help seeing himself."

"Does he lack self-understanding, though?" asked Caius. "He knows himself quite well, I'd say. He's just got more mirth in him than matter. He's way more dreamer than unformed doctor."

Justus glanced at Caius' hand, messily bandaged. "I wager that was Swift's doing?"

"He made quick work of a splinter."

Caius straightened the bandage.

"I'll give you that he has a caring instinct, but—"

"That isn't just care," said Justus. "It's empathy. Decisiveness. Presence. I believe that it's time for our dreamer to wake."

"Even on your ship, he'll find some way to dodge you," said Trystan.

Justus grinned.

"I'm counting on it."

~

SWIFT KNOTTED armfuls of whatever clothes happened to be scattered on his bed into a duffle bag.

He hooked on his small bedroll and pillow.

He clad himself in his thermo sailing suit, then pulled on his nylon trousers and windbreaker.

When he came back downstairs, he startled at finding Edric and Trystan rummaging through their suitcases, assembling duffle bags for overnight.

Caius came down the hall, wearing the sun-bleached bandana he always wore sailing, his own duffle bag hooked over his shoulder.

"Seems you rallied the troops."

Swift couldn't keep his smile subdued. "Seems so."

It didn't matter.

Caius was sneaking him a smile, too.

Mum bustled to him and peeked inside his bag. "Did you pack your warm gloves? I'd like you to have at least two changes of sailing clothes, plus a clean set for tomorrow's ride home. Do you have extra trousers? Not shorts. You'll need good shoes—no sandals, and no going barefoot on the boat."

"Not to worry, Mum." Swift zipped his bag, full of whatever he'd happened to stuff in, and slung its strap over his shoulder. "I've collected everything I ought."

He sauntered away from her, into the kitchen.

There, he drew out *The Star of Atlantis*—its map tucked inside, slid it into a plastic bag, and zipped it tight. He buttoned it fast inside his trouser pocket.

5

Stepping off the dock onto the *Regulus*—it was an immersion into an untamed world that fit Swift like a glove.

The treasure map buried in his pocket was the masterpiece of hundreds of adventures on this Celtic Sea, drawn by a hand now bone.

Swift slipped off his sandals and padded along the deck, the planks hard against his heels, the wood soaking warmth into him, the sun beating, heating him feet to face.

He unzipped his windbreaker as he stared up the mainmast, gazed along its knotted ropes, up and up into the fluttering main topgallant sail.

Trystan wasn't wrong that sailing would be difficult. Nothing about the sea was easy. Nothing about the ship was simple. The weather was tough, the currents unforgiving, the wind untamable.

But if he were to be any kind of treasure hunter, he had to harden himself to this.

He had to confront the challenges of the sea and try his stamina against the *Regulus*.

Taking in a sailing lesson from Justus, who put up with nothing less than full effort, was surely a good first step.

Not to mention, he wasn't just sailing today—he was going after the Star of Atlantis.

The *Regulus* was docked against a pier, tied along her portside with ropes that Caius was adjusting.

The starboard side was a plunge into the brink of the deeps, with beams of high sun shafting straight through the crystal blue water to the white-sanded seabed, a fathom below.

Swift crawled along the bench, staring into the translucent sea.

Keeping his gaze just over the gunwale, he felt like a shark stalking, unseen and unanticipated, circling a reef, back and forth, reserved—until a frenzy would strike and send him charging the deeps.

Swift glanced up. Edric and Trystan, priming the engine, were watching him.

He crouched and felt beneath the bench like he'd dropped something and was by no means trolling the fringes of the ship in shark persona.

Sharks on the Deck was an old game he and Ash used to play. He'd defaulted to it, that's all.

When Swift looked up again, Edric and Trystan had turned away and were helping Justus mind the lines on the foremast.

Justus loosed a rope, and the high, quadrilateral foresail released, then spread like a summer moon unfurling out of clouds.

The muscles in Swift's shoulders and back responded in kind, loosening.

Caius and Trystan tended the mainsail, then the mizzen.

It was as though their fingers, digging at knots and unstringing braided ropes from posts, were easing the tension in Swift's whole body.

Moments passed of the untying of everything, of the loosening of everything, of the freeing of everything.

Swift, feeling viscerally the unbinding of the ship,

reached a place where he was quite sure he himself was partly ship.

The openness of sea declared that anything was possible, and so he could very well be a descendent of a full-sized brigantine, or perhaps a galleon.

Maybe the ship commanded by the pirate who'd drawn his treasure map could somehow be his great-great-grandfather ship. Maybe the odd marks on the map were indeed words from an ancient language, not lost—but spoken by ships.

If all that were so, if in his bones and blood and tendons were coiled DNA strands of ship parts, he'd indeed be a natural at sailing. A born treasure-hunter.

Pacing the deck, he drew deep breaths, filling his lungs like they were two white topsails billowing. He stretched his arms as more ropes were divided from poles, feeling in his core the slow stirring of a ship waking—a stallion, refreshed from a cool night in a barn, strutting onto a golden field with not a fence in sight.

His gaze drifted off the starboard edge to a little jostling dinghy leashed to the ship. Here was the training boat he was to practice in today.

On her polished wooden hull, her name lay scrolled in pearly paint—"*Star Strider.*"

The *Strider* dancing in the water looked like a bucking colt, handling each surge with eccentricity and kicks—all drama—compared to the regal brigantine, heavy in the water, barely noticing the waves.

The *Strider*—it felt like his ship. Yes. The *Star Strider.* That was him.

The *Strider* had just a mainmast with a mainsail and a jib. Though sailing her wasn't simple, learning to manage her solo would be nothing compared to what his father would teach him on the *Regulus.*

The dinghy's sails, still hugging her poles, made Swift's spine feel clenched.

His fingers twitched to dig into those knots, to loosen the ropes himself.

Maybe he'd be allowed to sail the *Strider* right away.

Then he'd be experienced and could help work the *Regulus* 'til nightfall, pursuing the Star of Atlantis.

Swift drew out his book. He paged through nautical notes and, reaching the pirate verse, paused—

OF BEISHT KIONE, *the water wails,*
  I charge the deck and hoist the sails!
  The ship in kilt, Rusalka waits
  with dagger drawn to feed the fates.
  Yo Ho, Yo Ho – Drop the dead, and loose the stow!
  Yo Ho, Yo Ho – Into the darkness go.

THE SEA ALL BLACK, *the stars all drowned –*
  I strike the bloody colors down!
  The rain-rent sea – a cursed realm –
  Cthulhu calls – I take the helm.
  Yo Ho, Yo Ho – Fight the waves and keel the foe!
  Yo Ho, Yo Ho – Over the waves we go.

THE MORNING BREAKS *– I look to sea,*
  to where the storm has ferried me.
  Mine eyes deceive! But no – there be:
  Atlantis' Star heaved from the deeps!
  Yo Ho, Yo Ho – Swab the deck and lash the tow!
  Yo Ho, Yo Ho – To Brandy Brook we go!

THE BEISHT KIONE, a horse-headed, foul creature, whom real Welsh fishermen he'd talked to actually feared, swam into Swift's mind around the Kraken-toothed islet, hissing mist, as savvy Grog Blossom sidled in, a rusty double-musket raised.

The Cthulhu—the Old One—Dragon, tentacled, armed with ink and poison, ascended from the depths of Swift's imagination and snuck its claws around the Star of Atlantis.

A Rusalka maiden—beautiful, bright-eyed, and long dead, eased onto a moony shore in a dark corner of Swift's mind, the shining flat of a dagger clenched between her teeth.

And Swift envisioned mermaids blending in the distant blue, waiting for the dark to fall so they could slip near to shore.

He unfolded the map and studied it. He glanced up, comparing the coast to what lay drawn before him.

Edric was right that the Wentletrap was enormous, and that the cove drawn here was certainly not to scale and might be one of hundreds.

But—the beach spreading from the dock was perfectly straight, and to the north it tended craggy. There was a cove up there, certainly.

They were docked at the Wentletrap's very southernmost edge, its trees heaving along shallow hills. The forest went on for miles up the coast, deepening and thickening as it stretched further north.

The map was drawn just the same—a straight beach, dotted with round boulders, edging the Wentletrap; and then a stretch of water broken by a jagged sea wall jetting out to form the southern hook of a cove.

Looking north toward those enclosing shore rocks, map in hand, was like seeing a face, not recognized, transform into a familiar guise—like a friend remembered from an old school.

"That's got to be Sterncastle Cove."

Swift folded his map and stowed it in its book. He tucked the book inside its plastic bag and slipped it into his pocket.

Against his thigh, it felt heavy as a plank of deck wood; a block of real, Welsh maritime history, spilling secrets.

He crossed the deck to his brothers and father, adjusting the ropes on the mast. "Seems the treasure could lie in that cove to the north. Can we head northward as you teach me sailing?"

Justus handed him a life jacket. "The wind we're catching, leading west, is steady. Best we keep the *Regulus* true to west for your first lesson."

Swift tipped his chin toward those gorgeous white waters slooshing around the charcoal rocks rimming the southern tip of the cove—Sterncastle Cove, maybe. "The treasure's got to be north."

Justus glanced at the cove. "Those northern waters look a bit tough."

Swift patted his pocket. "Isn't the treasure why we're here, though? I mean—once I learn to sail?"

Justus opened the trap door to the galley. "Learning to sail is the work of a lifetime. If you're to make a beginning today, shouldn't you commit to the task at hand?"

The steeled resolve in Justus' eyes told Swift the question was rhetorical.

Swift backed off, shaking down his hunch that he was actually part ship and might not really need to commit to the task at hand to gain mastery of this.

Smiling just to himself, he drew on his life jacket.

He kept clear of his brothers as they bustled about the center deck.

They had no idea what they were in for. He was going to be so capable—a natural at everything.

They'd see him perform perfectly on the dinghy, then they'd take the *Regulus* to open water, catch the steady wind and work their vessel north, and Swift would scout his treasure.

Come nightfall, when they were camping underneath the starry Pembrokeshire skies, reveling in a hoard of wealth, this would be the talk:

How is Swift so naturally good with ships? He's amazing! Caius would say, wearing a king's silver crown.

He's really grown up a lot, Edric would say, sitting on a silver chest of diamonds and pearls Swift would've let him borrow.

All I've mastered is cider and the cello, and my thirteen-

year-old brother is a master sailor and treasure finder! Trystan would say, serving up dinner on golden plates.

I've never seen any lad more suited for the sea, nor quicker at learning something so impossibly difficult, Justus would say, standing over Swift, who'd be modest-looking, nestled warm beneath Neptune's actual blue cloak, thoughtfully adding his venture to the record of voyages written in *The Star of Atlantis.*

"Swift," called Justus. "Mind what your brothers are doing."

Swift drew his gaze off the cove. "Can I help with anything?"

"The sails must first be fixed for setting off. Watch your brothers."

Swift's fingers twitched. "Maybe you could teach me what they're doing, then I could fix the sails for setting off."

A small smile dawned on Justus. "Your dose of teaching is imminent."

"But I could be helpful," said Swift.

"Go and sit down," said Edric. "You'll have your paws on rope and canvas soon enough."

Swift knelt on the bench at the tip of the bow.

He tried to watch his brothers work but couldn't help glancing off to scan the distant sea for flashes of kraken tentacles and mermaid fins. All he saw, though, were waves.

He peered straight down into the crystalline water, gently rocking the *Regulus.*

On the sea floor scuttled crabs—big, ten-legged things, red as anger, defending territory lines Swift couldn't track.

Crabs had always troubled him a bit, not because they were spidery or clawed, but because they were merciless.

One crab, straight below the boat, had just gone through a molt. Its shell was pink—not red—and fingernail thin.

Molting crabs were skittish, light-bodied things. They were difficult to see and catch; more compelled to run and hide than a crab with a hardened shell.

A red-shelled crab had caught sight of the molting one and was advancing.

"Bug off," Swift told it.

The words seemed to bounce off the water and disappear into wind.

The bully crab was feasting—half a fish hung out of its mouth. The molting one was gripping something fleshy in its tender claw. Knowing what would happen next, Swift tried to look away, but couldn't.

The red monster took a stab at the weak one, seizing its hard-earned kill and skating away.

The victim crab, pathetic in its unfired skin, drifted up into a current from the blow.

Swift watched the pale crab swirl into a heap of rocks.

"Are we doing this today, or what?"

Swift spun to find Edric right behind him.

"Justus has been calling you," said Edric, his hand on his hip, his eyes a bit scary and wide.

"I didn't hear." Swift came away from the bench.

"You're going to have to listen better. Justus doesn't say things twice."

Swift knew. He hurried to his father.

Justus took a seat on the deck stairs. He handed Swift a guide on sails.

Swift flipped through it, his fascination, his longing for mastery of seamanship, for nautical treasure-hunting, seeming to drop a taproot in his chest.

Justus moved over a little as Swift sat down by him. "We'll review the basics, let you have a tour of the canvas and lines, and then you'll spend the afternoon trimming the sails of the *Regulus* and the *Star Strider*. If there's time, I'll let you pilot the *Strider* seaward a ways and back, exercising your technique with her sails."

With the groan the wind was coaxing from the brigantine's masts—its topsails practically reaching the clouds—the magnitude of the towering ship seemed overwhelming.

But a ship's deck was a stage so tough that red crabs might as well hovel here.

It was no place to admit intimidation.

"Why do I just get to trim the sails?" Swift sat taller. "Won't I need to practice with all the other ropes and things, on open water as we go, if I'm to learn?"

"Father would never turn a thirteen-year-old loose on his *Regulus*." Edric tossed Swift's duffle bag down to Trystan, in the berth.

"I was drinking before he let me have a real go at sailing," said Trystan.

Justus slipped on reading glasses and handed Swift a guide on lines. "We'll first use the sheet to trim the sail. Then we'll set out a mile or so, and you can fuss with the ropes to experiment with the wind as you fine tune the tautness and angle of each sail."

"When I'm in the *Strider*, may I sail her north?"

"Think not so much of sailing the *Strider* as angling her sails," said Justus. "Your purpose today is to grow accustomed to the feel of the wind—when it's calm and when it's perturbed. Maintaining a balance and keeping course will be your occupation, more than gaining distance or a destination. Today you shall develop a good understanding, a healthy respect, of water and wind."

Angling sails all afternoon wasn't anything close to Swift's idea of mastering sailing. Or gearing up for treasure hunting.

Justus' teaching tended to involve practicing ad nauseam, and if this were the way of it, they'd never finish to set off and search for the Star of Atlantis.

He kept himself calm. Kept himself focused on Justus. Maybe if he did really well at trimming the sails of the *Regulus*, they'd seat him in the *Strider* early. He'd get to unfurl that delicious rope with his own fingers, loose her knots, flair her wide and slight, just like Justus and the others had done on the *Regulus*.

Then Swift could work the sail assigned to him on the big ship and help pilot her flawlessly, convincing Justus that he'd learned everything—a feat that could be rewarded with a chance to make for the treasure, with lots of daylight left.

Justus nodded to Caius, standing by the mainmast.

Caius walked among the ropes and pointed. "Halyard rope. Outhaul tension. Traveler adjustment. Boom vang tension." He pointed to the sails and named each one.

Justus glanced at Swift. "Can you repeat that?"

Swift had heard the labels many times, and today they seemed especially to be sticking.

He went to each bit of line and canvas, pointing and naming.

"Well done." Justus joined him at the mainmast and demonstrated methods of trimming the sail. "Trimming the sail is your most important skill. The smallest of adjustments can make a big impact on how a ship manages wind."

Edric climbed onto the starboard rail.

He caught the rope of the *Strider*, rocking gently in the water, and yanked her near. He dropped into her.

Swift jumped away from Justus. "That's my ship." He darted to the bow.

Edric mastered his balance in the *Strider*, then set to loosening the lovely ropes, flaring her pale mainsail with his meaty fists.

Edric met Swift's stare. "She's not your ship." He reached to the bow and unbound the jib.

All the wind in Swift blew out. Edric wasn't learning. He was.

"Mind you," called Justus. "Don't set the lines too firm for the lad. "Better not to agitate him with knots unnecessarily tight."

Edric was ignoring Swift glaring at him, so Swift turned his glare onto Caius.

Caius rested his hand on Swift's shoulder. "Can't ever trust the deck hands, can you?"

Swift narrowed his eyes at Edric, climbing up the ropes and straddling the rail back onto the *Regulus*. "Bilge-sucking deck hands."

"If you were to drop into the dinghy now"—Justus drew Swift back to the mainmast—"you'd be clumsy with her sails."

Swift held back. "I'm better at this than you think."

His body had already mastered the cadence of the *Regulus'* swaying. His two feet planted felt like masts themselves.

"You might be the very best at this," said Justus. "Still, the *Regulus* has muscle that will try you and loosen you up. After you've spent some time with her, mastering the temper of the *Strider* will feel like a holiday. Even further out on open sea."

The fluttering of the *Strider's* mainsail was seduction.

Swift eased to the starboard rail.

"I've watched you sail so much." Not to mention, he'd sat in the dinghy loads of times with a brother and was very good at balancing it. "Let me in the *Star Strider*, just for a minute, by myself."

The dinghy looked tiny in the water.

It looked simple. Easy. Even dumb.

"Just let me try."

Caius guided Swift back to the mast. "You're better off listening to Justus."

Swift jerked away. "What do you know about it?" His fists clenched.

Losing himself to an outburst, when he knew it wouldn't help his case, frustrated him more than his father's refusal, more than the look of enjoyment on Edric's face—so pleased, it seemed, with his payoff for the agitation he'd dealt.

Caius bent until his eyes were even with Swift's.

The posture, meant to be kind, made Swift feel like a tiny child—simple and so small.

"Justus won't have you handle what you aren't ready for," said Caius. "This is how we all learned. You'll practice trimming each sail, while he coaches you. Handling the *Strider* solo will come next."

Swift glanced at Edric, full on grinning now.

Probably, he was imagining that once Swift started in on trimming the *Regulus*, he'd be sweating, rope-burned, and humiliated in a matter of ten minutes.

If that happened, Edric wouldn't just grin. He'd laugh if Swift went weak and sank to the bench. And Justus would catch Edric's glance and smirk.

"You think I need baby steps?"

Swift's fists felt strong as deck wood.

He certainly carried splinters and rope hull in his marrow.

"I could handle the *Regulus*, no problem. It's just that I want to pilot the *Star Strider* first."

Claiming it, red-faced, in front of Edric, felt so good.

"If you lose your temper, lad, the lesson's done," said Justus. "I'll deposit you in the beach house with your mum while your brothers and I sail and camp."

The threat was not empty. And if he lost his temper because Edric had pushed him over the brink of frustration, the punishment still would be his alone. He needed to get ahold of himself.

Swift kept his eyes on the dinghy, prancing in the water, until the threat of the consequence cooled.

He could certainly handle the dinghy. There was absolutely no question. If they'd just let him work her now, he'd muster some respect before trying his hand at the hard-horned brigantine.

Then, even if she did wear him out, there'd at least be a layer of self-respect to insulate him from Edric's jabs and Justus' half-smiles.

Swift loosened his fists so Justus would see he was fully in control.

He straightened his spine and steadied his voice. "Let me in the *Strider* for just a minute. Let me trim her sail one time."

Justus was watching him, one brow raised.

This was an invitation to keep talking. He was waiting for an argument. A good one.

Swift thought about the word *rhetoric* as he stated, "Edric did such a nice job setting the tension of the *Strider's* sails just right. If I don't take advantage of that now, the wind will have tightened the knots, and they'll be impossible to loosen."

"Oh, let the lad have a go," said Edric, arms crossed.

Swift stared at him. Why would Edric be taking his side?

"He wants in the *Strider* now, and I'm all for it." The grin still marred Edric's face.

Swift glimpsed Caius catching their father's eye and shaking his head.

More arguments stacked up inside of Swift—all the points Justus had made this morning, about Swift's capabilities. Justus might've read them without Swift having to say anything because he was shifting, foot to foot.

Swift looked up at him. "I can do it. I know I can."

Justus laid his arm around Swift's shoulders and guided him to the rail. "If you must have the *Strider*, then you must."

Caius advanced. "He's not ready."

Swift threw him a dirty look.

Caius was supposed to be supporting him, but he seemed to have forgotten that. Why would Caius not want Swift to earn a moment of early success?

Edric climbed back over the rail and scaled down the net on the side of the ship. He landed again in the *Strider*.

Caius took hold of Swift's lifejacket and zipped it.

Swift shrugged off his hands and followed Edric's course down the ropes.

Edric reached to steady him, the way Caius often did.

Swift cautiously held out his hand for Edric to take.

Edric took Swift's wrist and spotted him until he found purchase on the *Strider's* bench.

Edric unbound the rope anchoring the *Strider* to the big ship. He climbed back onto the ship's netting.

Grinning, he shoved the little craft away. "She's all yours."

Swift clung to her mast.

The *Strider*, released from the *Regulus*, leapt with each rapid wave, and through her body, Swift could feel the gently beating sea.

An impression struck him of the summer when he turned eleven, when he first had tried an English saddle. After learning on a bulky western, an English felt like riding bareback—nothing divided his thighs from the power of the horse.

The current was keeping the *Strider* near to the *Regulus*, but even so, Swift felt the sense of release.

He threaded his hand into his pocket and touched the corners of his book beneath its plastic.

He was sitting even with the very sea drawn on his map. And just north lay that white-watered cove, possibly caging the Star of Atlantis.

The track of sea stretching to the cove looked like a country of sapphire hills, treasure-laden. The brine mist, stinging his eyes and dusting his skin with salt wind, summoned tears.

The climbing sun—cascading warmth through the chill air and filling each wave peak with light—seemed an echo of the treasure, lost in these bright waters, waiting for Swift. For the brilliant sun, too, was a star.

Above him, his father and brothers stared down.

"Do just as I say," called Justus. "Not a smidgen more, not a smidgen less."

Swift met his father's eyes. He nodded. He was more than ready.

"Edric has fixed the mainsail with a mezzo-slackness that's good for high-winded days," said Justus. "But on a gentler day like this, you want it more firm than slack. Do you understand?"

"I do," Swift hollered up.

"Carefully, loosen the knot at the base of the mainsail. Then slide it along the boom, straight toward the stern. Slowly."

Swift found the knot—the delicious knot. He tunneled his fingers in until it gave. He pushed it marginally toward the stern.

The wind swelled the sail. Moved the *Strider*.

Swift shivered at the miracle of the vessel responding to his advance, the way a gentled stallion might.

"Very good," called Justus.

Swift kept his eyes on the bright sail, his face toward the dazzling sea, so they wouldn't see his absurd grin.

"Give her a little more now," called Justus. "Go bit by bit. Feel the change in the play of the wind as you ease broad the sail."

Swift pushed the knot and felt it catch.

The wood of the boom was swollen here.

He tried to force the knot across the wood, but it wouldn't slip. He crouched closer to the rope, tried to work free the loop.

It wouldn't ease, and it wouldn't budge.

He leaned into it with both hands.

"Easy," called Justus. "Nudge, don't press."

Swift backed up, meeting the knot eye to eye like it was a stubborn colt. He lunged at it, two handed, throwing all his weight.

The knot moved and came undone all at once. The wind kicked in and bloated the sail.

"The rope," cried Justus. "Take it!"

Swift leapt for the rope, but the wind was quicker and whipped it out of reach.

In a flash, the sail was free and billowing like the breast of a rearing horse. A wave smashed in and heaved the hull.

The *Strider* leapt, throwing Swift.

Swift heard the smack of the water before he felt it.

Before he really knew what had happened, he was sinking, clawing at the skim.

His life jacket bobbed him to the surface.

He tried to breathe but couldn't—he'd taken the boom rod straight to the chest, square between his lifejacket's plates.

A high wave coursed in.

It swallowed him.

He worked to open his eyes against the salt and found himself tumbling head down over the rippling seabed, spangled with the sharp-red shells of crabs.

A strong hand gripped his ankle. A yank and a flip, and he was in arms and rising toward the sunlit surface.

When he broke the skim, he gasped a breath, but his diaphragm was frozen—he couldn't let the air back out.

"Don't struggle." Caius, calm and firm, gripping him strongly, held Swift on the top of the waves.

Swift went limp and let the sea float him, let his head rest on Caius' shoulder.

"You're okay," said Caius. "Trystan's lowering the board."

Swift opened his eyes to see the white rescue board dropping from the *Regulus*. He glimpsed Justus, in the water too, catching the board and swimming it over.

"Don't be afraid," said Caius. "I've got you."

The turbulence of seawater around him, in him, under him—he felt dandled by raw power; allied with something fierce.

Resting against Caius, both of them cresting and troughing with incoming waves—it was like they were riding the shoulders of a giant.

He closed his eyes and let the sea teach him its strength; let his memory relive the mighty heave that'd bucked the *Strider*.

"I don't think he's all the way awake," said Caius.

Swift wanted to say he was awake, that he could climb onto the board by himself. But breaths weren't coming easy, and all he could do was squeak.

A moment later, they had him strapped on, and he was riding up the flank of the *Regulus*.

Trystan pulled him over the rail and loosed the straps. "Can you breathe?"

Swift, gasping, couldn't speak. But he could sit up on his own.

Caius and Justus scaled the ropes and slipped over the rail like two bedraggled water rats, seawater seeping out their trouser legs and draining from their sleeves.

Trystan stripped off Swift's lifejacket and windbreaker.

Caius peeled off Swift's soaked thermo suit, draped him with a towel, and rubbed him.

Caius glanced at Edric, sitting on the bench, just staring. "Make yourself useful and find him something warm."

Edric rose and returned a moment later, holding Swift's

duffle bag open and rummaging through. "Warm. Well, there's underpants in here. Lots. Three pairs of pajama bottoms. A couple of dirty shirts. Some random socks. Anyone bring something warm that would fit the lad?"

Justus slipped Swift's wet trousers off, dried his legs, and snugged a pair of fleece pajama bottoms onto him. "Get him a sweater from my bag."

Swift's chest had stopped smarting, and the paralysis gripping his middle was easing, letting him have whole breaths.

He reached to the trousers his father had set aside and dug in the pocket for his book. It was still dry in its plastic bag.

"Want me to haul in the *Strider* before we go?" asked Trystan, "Or can we keep her docked and leave her by the *Regulus*?"

"Leave her?" Swift hugged his book. "We can't go. I haven't learned anything."

Caius leaned down. "We'll come again another day."

"No." Swift pushed away from him. "I only got the wind knocked out of me is all."

The big rolls rocking beneath them now, gently, on the sea-strong *Regulus*, were an intoxication.

"You almost drowned," said Caius.

"I didn't almost drown. You saw to that."

Caius glanced at Justus. "We ought to call it a day. Come back when we're fresh."

Swift tugged his father's sleeve. "Teach me a lesson on the *Regulus*. I promise I won't argue. And I'll listen and need instructions only one time."

He'd loved the sea for as long as he could remember. But to experience its power like that—it was like, in the moment the *Strider* bucked him, he'd drawn back a veil of wind and waves and found the face of a startled god.

"Please."

Edric shook his head. "I thought we established that begging like a baby's not your thing."

Caius moved in Edric's face. "And grumbling like an old hag isn't yours."

Worse than the chill of the wind on his wet skin, worse than the stinging from the strike of the boom rod, Swift smarted at having been foolish enough to team with Edric; to imagine all that encouragement had been a sign that he cared.

"Caius. Edric." Justus stood. "This was no one's fault. It was an unlucky buck."

Justus rarely found fault with Edric. And when he did, he was quick to excuse.

Caius jabbed Edric's chest. "You saw this coming, and so did I. But you egged it on." He gestured to Swift. "Did you want your little brother drowned?"

Edric pushed him away. Caius shoved back.

"Enough." Justus divided Caius and Edric. "Swift, I'm willing to keep on the water. But if this keeps up, I'll drop the two of you together in the *Strider* and let you manage your own way home."

Swift pushed to his knees. "Are you serious? You'll let me stay?"

Justus peeled Swift's towel off him and examined a bruise forming on his ribs.

"That was quite a blow you took. Are you in pain?"

Swift glanced down at the red bruise, bright on his chest. "Not much."

Justus felt around the bruise without Swift wincing. "If you're willing, I see no reason we can't keep at it." He took a bone-white sweater Trystan was holding and snugged it over Swift's head. "Wouldn't be a proper lesson, I suppose, without someone getting wet."

Swift stood, reeling.

Justus' expectations were always high, and it was clear Swift was pleasing him by wanting to keep on.

There'd been a time when the pressure to persist in a lesson with Justus would've been draining.

But now he seemed to understand his father a bit more. Justus might have some heritage of seas and ships inside him, same as Swift.

And so perhaps he still had a bent for treasure hunting.

He wanted to keep going with Swift.

He'd said that to the others.

Even after what happened, he saw Swift's venture as worthwhile.

Swift rubbed his chest—smarting, but in a good way, like the pang of stretching a newly worked muscle. He'd just handled a challenge that would've benched most kids his age.

Ash certainly couldn't have taken a buck like that and gotten back to his feet.

But here was Swift, on the calm side of a confrontation with the sea that'd bruised him, but not wrecked him.

For a flash, he saw in himself—if only a little—what Justus might see.

And that vision of potential, of competence, would carry him on—on to even rougher seas, on to the north. On to the sea's bounty, waiting for him.

Swift walked to Justus. "What would you like me to do?"

The approach was the offering of a pact—a glimmer of what pirate treasure, ships, and seas were all about; a thirst for saltwater and wind; a willingness to muscle up against the pressure of lines and sails for the chance of something magnificent happening. Even with a bruising rib.

Especially with a bruising rib.

Justus completed the pact by handing Swift a coiled rope. "Today is all about gaining respect for water and wind. An understanding of the deeps. You'll first trim the *Regulus'* mainsail on open water. Watch how it's done." He glanced at Trystan. "Take us west a mile, then kill the engine. We'll give the lad a taste of Celtic wind."

6

Swift lifted his hand into the current of wind and gathered a sense of its bearing.

Justus, though still watching him, had joined Trystan and Edric, sitting at the stern, more than an hour ago.

Swift eyed the telltales on each sail up the mainmast, spotted a flutter in the highest one, and pressed the block forward.

The *Regulus*, the great, strong *Regulus Borealis*, moved.

The ship's strutting—from the power Swift had harnessed—was as steady as if there'd been a burst of fuel from the engine.

"That's it," said Justus, now approaching.

Caius, seeing to the sails on the foremast, called from across the ship, "Nice."

Justus gazed up at the billowing sails.

"You've got a winning day for this. The wind couldn't be any steadier."

"Then let's sail north. That cove's not far." Swift dashed to the bow. "With a wind this good and how we're catching it, we'd reach Sterncastle Cove in a quarter hour."

They'd meandered far enough westward that Swift could

see not just the outcropping rocks of Sterncastle Cove, but the curve they made, sweeping in.

The cove was almost completely enclosed by those rocks, but there was a clear sightline in, through a passage at the southern crook, where the rocks broke square and even.

The water there was frothy-white, with eddies swirling, making a gateway. And beyond that, inside the cove, the waves softened to near stillness.

With the sun cresting straight above, raining glitter onto the sea from a blue topaz sky, it was easy to see how some sailors really believed in mermaid lagoons. Sterncastle Cove's water looked glassy and sparkling.

It was a perfect place for the Star of Atlantis to rest.

Swift glanced back at Justus. "If Trystan and Edric helped, if we all worked the *Regulus* together, we might reach the cove faster."

Justus gazed past Swift into the entrance of the cove.

If Swift himself had been born centuries ago, as the pirate he sometimes imagined he was, he couldn't think of a better place on any coast to stow a treasure.

The way Justus was gazing at the cove, maybe he, too, was feeling its invitation. Maybe he was longing to explore it, as Swift was, and would even declare the lesson finished.

Maybe he'd let Trystan fire the engine and just hurry them right to it.

"No, lad." Justus waved Swift down from where he'd climbed onto the rail. "A change of course would fracture your momentum. You're doing very well."

He handed Swift back the line. "Keep at it. Keep us moving. I'd like to see more consistent control. Your tension's still flagging in the bottom telltale of the main."

Swift held taut the line and moved the block back while Justus retreated again to the stern.

~

SWIFT SPENT the sunniest part of the afternoon with the main, learning to keep a high level of tension as the gale crescendoed and eased.

Of all the sails he'd worked so far, he liked the mainmast best.

The mainmast was easy to talk to, and it listened well, its response almost immediate, its silky line gliding along its block as though oiled.

If he worked it just right, he could keep the tower of sails all together cradling wind, pulling the *Regulus*.

That old Welsh marooner, Bartholomew Roberts, hailed in his library books on Celtic piracy—he couldn't have done any better himself.

Ash certainly couldn't have done better.

Keeping his eye on the horizon, feeling the wind bridled by his own hands, Swift could even imagine he was on Roberts' ship.

Or better, his own ship!

He'd be Captain Corkscrew—what Ash used to call him in their games—and he'd see his crew of jolly buccaneers through storms to waiting treasure.

After another half hour, Justus came back to the deck and inspected Swift's arcing sails.

"You're doing well," said Justus. "Strikingly well. I imagined you'd be ready to call it a day after half so many attempts. But here you are, standing strong, your mainmast sails full of wind."

Swift's breathing quickened. It was like his father's words were billowing him.

Perhaps Justus was seeing Swift—on a ship—as the competent lad that he wanted to see.

And maybe he was beginning to admit what Swift already knew: Swift was born to the sea, to the wilds, to adventure—more, perhaps, than he was born to medicine.

So, perhaps Justus would soon conclude that Swift had bided his time and was due the reward of some treasure hunting.

"If you feel up to it, I'd allow you another try in the *Strider*," said Justus.

Swift dropped the line. "You're letting me back in?"

Justus picked up the rope and tied it off. "A sailor must not be defeated by a single buck." He led Swift to the rail. "The *Star Strider* is manageable for you, at your level, but don't misinterpret my confidence. She's a little vessel but not easy to pilot solo."

Caius spotted Swift—climbing over the rail.

This time, now that Swift had earned his father's confidence, Edric was nowhere nearby to lend encouragement or help, or even to hear. He was just eyeing Swift from the stern.

If Swift didn't know better, he'd think Edric's face seemed to betray some concern.

"The *Strider* will test your stamina," said Justus. "Your balance. Steady force is required to keep her moving true. You'll soon see for yourself."

Swift, more than up for the task, spidered down the net and hopped right into the little boat. "Can I take her anywhere I want?"

Justus unhooked the *Strider's* ropes from the Brigantine's hull. "You'll sail straight west, using the same wind you've been catching here."

Swift gave Sterncastle Cove another quick glance but let go of the fight rising in him to reach it. More arguing at this point could lose him his chance to be on the *Strider* at all.

"Go easy with her," said Justus. "Avoid the rough-handed approach. Aim to feel the difference of the wind's draw on a simpler set of sails."

Edric's face, lit with its smirk, appeared over the rail between their father and Caius. "You know what girls say about rough-handed sailors?"

Caius elbowed him. "Would you leave him alone?"

"What? I'm just trying to lighten things. Isn't that what you asked me to do?"

Swift found he could ignore Edric, no problem. If Edric

meant to intimidate, he'd chosen his moment poorly. Justus had been singing Swift's praises.

And Swift was ready for this. Justus knew it and had said so.

Now Edric would watch Swift try again, and it'd be a much better try than before.

Swift studied the boom, his mind tracing his misstep.

Touching the swollen wood, a tenderness seemed to have woken in his fingers.

He assessed the knot, determining the right level of strength to apply.

A twist—a very gentle twist—was all that was needed. He'd been too forceful with it before. That's what he'd done wrong.

It seemed, now, he could conceive in his muscles and bones how delicate each adjustment had to be to keep the sail under control.

He picked up the line.

He looked up at his father.

Justus nodded.

In one fluid push, he broadened the sail perfectly.

A wave received the boat from the wind and drew the *Strider* away from the *Regulus*.

Swift kept the trim taut as wind churned steady in the sail.

Before he knew it, the *Regulus* lay behind him, diminished, its four watching sailors shrinking on the bow.

7

*J*ustus settled his hands in his pockets, pride pulling his smile wide. "Look at the lad go." He glanced at Caius. "I'd say that's my son."

Caius didn't take his eyes off Swift. "No doubt."

"Want me in the steering deck?" asked Trystan.

"Keep her idling," said Justus. "In case we need to swoop in."

"*In case,*" said Edric. "You mean *when.*"

"He's getting the knack," said Justus. "He's gaining a sense of his capabilities."

"When do you plan on pinning him?" asked Edric.

"Is that all you care about?" Caius asked him. "Did you come here to help Swift, or only to watch Father deal with him?"

"It isn't that I don't care," said Edric. "But someone's got to show the lad that the world won't coddle him, the way you do."

"When he's good and worn, I'll approach him," said Justus, keeping his eyes on the challenging waves.

On his lad riding them.

"I'll recognize the fertile moment when it arrives."

"You sure medicine's his cup of tea?" asked Trystan.

"I mean—I see the same stirrings of interest we noted in Caius. But..."

"But it takes quite a bit more than interest," said Caius.

"You can't argue that Swift hasn't the intelligence, the discipline to one day handle the kind of training you're in," said Justus. "Surely."

"It takes more than intelligence and discipline, too," said Caius. "To get through the misery of training, he'd have to love medicine."

"You don't think he loves it?" asked Justus.

Caius shrugged. "He likes it, maybe. I don't know about love. You start him now in that Practicum, he'll need enough enthusiasm to carry him through a dozen years of heavy lifting."

"Can you not see it?" Justus asked Trystan, sitting behind the wheel. "Can you not perceive Swift as a born medical doctor?"

"He's brilliant," said Trystan. "But he likes to play. And he likes having time to himself. I've always seen him as a bit of a late bloomer."

"Trystan's nailed it," said Edric. "If Swift ever were to get serious about something like medicine, it'd probably be too late for him to have any shot at making it. I mean, when I think of a young prodigy medical student, I don't think of Swift. Don't most kids like that grow obsessed with academics rather than legends?"

"I'd say Swift is pretty obsessed with academics," said Trystan. "He's into far higher maths than any of us were at thirteen. And he speaks seven languages, right?"

"Eight," said Caius.

On the water, this far out, Swift's height made him look a few years older than he was. Watching him through binoculars showed him doing everything right.

Swift never let his focus flag. He stayed cognizant of the force and direction of the wind. When Swift was faced with a choice, Justus could almost read his thoughts, sharp and fluid, delivering him to the optimal course.

His thin body was sinewy and quick under his life jacket, his hands obedient and nimble in the frigid wind.

"You're all but seeing him in that Practicum, aren't you?" asked Caius.

Justus handed him the binoculars. "Young as the lad is, you must admit how he engages when you're on about your classes. That's uncommon."

"Well, yes, but the way medicine runs in our family, he's bound to harbor some interest."

"He always wants to see what you're studying," said Justus. "He presses you to explain it. And the questions he asks are great ones. No doubt as good, if not better than what some of your fellows could formulate."

And in Swift, a deep love of caring for others was germinating. Anytime someone was hurt or ill, Swift was markedly quick to act. And his empathy was palpable. It'd strongly manifested a few years ago when Swift happened upon a dying fox in their oak woods.

"Do you see it in him?" Trystan asked Caius. "This destiny to dive into medicine?"

"If you ask me, it's too early to pin him. But—I'm no father." Caius glanced at Justus. "You steered us right. I think the real question is whether you'll manage wresting the lad's mind away from other matters. His dreaming of ocean adventure was abstract until he laid his hands on that book."

"He won't be a lad for much longer," said Justus.

"True," said Caius. "But in driving him toward the Practicum, you're asking for the rest of his childhood."

"There's also the matter of his fox," said Justus. "We mustn't forget what we saw that night."

"Oh, yes." Caius lowered the binoculars. "I'll never forget —seeing him in such distress."

It was a young fox Swift had found, injured, lying close to death in the woods behind their home.

The lad sat with the fox for a whole evening, trying to comfort him, offering him water. The gestures won him the animal's trust in his final hour.

When night fell, the poor creature pulled himself near, laid his chin on Swift's knee, and passed.

Caius and Justus, beside themselves with worry, finally hunted Swift down an hour after dark. They found him in pieces and tears, cradling the dead fox.

"Was that distress?" asked Justus. "Or love?"

Caius didn't answer.

Justus took back the binoculars and watched Swift.

The lad's sailing had a style to it, even this early in training. His management of the *Strider* wasn't rigid. It was like he felt the sea and went with it, improvising along with whatever it dealt.

That flexibility earned him more bounty in distance than what a by-the-book sailor might achieve.

"He'll do well in medicine," said Justus. "That mind. That presence. That stamina. Yes, very well."

"That bullheadedness," said Edric. "If you ask me, he's not one to stuff into a mold."

When it came to Swift, Edric had always been insightful.

Edric saw Swift differently—dealt with him differently—than the rest of them. Since the day Swift was born, Edric kept back his warmth.

He did like Swift, in his way. He just demanded that Swift earn what was given, which was generally good for the lad. Edric was certainly right that Swift danced to his own drum.

But Caius, too, was right—an older brother can't easily see a lad as the man he'll become.

But a father can.

"Think of such a one in an operating room," said Justus. "Imagine—how quick his hands, how much quicker, his thinking. After such an experience, such education as I'd like him in—why, he could turn on a dime and handily manage any scattered crisis of Caius' trauma wing."

"This has always been your dream for him, hasn't it?" asked Trystan. "That he'd one day follow you."

Was Swift not, indeed, the son most similar to himself? "You believe I'm wishing to see myself in the lad?"

"Just a trap to be mindful of," said Trystan.

"I see quite a lot of myself in the lad," said Edric. "I'm glad you're set on cornering him today. Whether it's medicine or something else that catches his eye, he needs a push to start thinking about who he is." He moved away from the rail. "Like it or not, he isn't cut and dry like the rest of you."

"I might not be as cut and dry as you think," said Justus. "When I was Swift's age, I was more obsessed than even he with treasure and sailing adventures."

"You're joking," said Trystan.

"I'm quite serious," said Justus. "When I was a boy, a rumor spread that someone had discovered the Star of Atlantis. The whole thing was hogwash—a prank. But the hype popularized the treasure, and soon every child near the Welsh Coast was dreaming of taking it."

"Is it real, do you think?" asked Caius.

Justus chuckled. "There's hope in your eyes, son. But of course there is. You're my lad, too."

"You're not saying Swift's treasure could really be out there, surely," said Edric.

"I believe it has to be a true piece of maritime history, yes," said Justus. "As a lad myself, I lived near an old sailor kind enough to take me out looking from time to time. Despite that we both reckoned it to be long lost, the chase was quite thrilling."

"What if you left Swift alone for a while?" asked Caius. "Would he not discover medicine on his own, if it were right for him?"

"He perhaps would," said Justus. "But he'd miss the chance to go after the Practicum. I'll not allow that."

"Father's right to check him." Edric, staring at the lad, was marked by a rare shade of tenderness. "It'll be kind to do him the favor of fixing his feet square on the ground before his heart's broken."

Indeed, Edric did care for Swift. Though his approach was a rough one, he, too, was teaching his brother.

Caius, watching Swift with them, looked not a bit tender.

Rather, he was white knuckled, his face strained as he fixed on the lad, way out, teetering in the *Strider* atop a big wave.

Justus raised his binoculars to his eyes.

Swift shifted his weight.

Balanced the craft.

Adjusted the sail to steady the ship's rocking.

He was fine.

The look on Swift's face was one he wore when he went at chemistry schoolwork. It was a twisted brow—a mind full of strategies, of solutions; eyes full of calculation.

"He's suited to medicine more than he can imagine." Justus glanced at his other sons. "More than any of us can imagine, I'll wager."

SWIFT TRAINED his gaze on his father, his brothers, as he guided the *Strider* to turn and square with the *Regulus*.

Justus shouted, "Well done." His words, though barely audible over the wind, sent a thrill up Swift's spine. "Steer her to portside."

Swift let the pressure off the mainsail.

The wind evaporated like an escaped dove. The relieved sail fluttered as Swift pried the oar from the stow and steadied the craft.

He tightened the sail again and aimed for the *Regulus'* portside.

The wind responded true, and his sailing in was a promenade, his brothers watching, his father's mouth held open in a smile.

Even Edric looked a bit proud, though he seemed to be trying to mask it, glancing down as he was.

Though the *Strider* kept to her course, moving eastward

now—the wind felt like a different species than what Swift had been working. It took all his attentiveness to each gust to keep the telltales in check.

But he did it.

And reaching the big ship's hull, letting the *Strider's* sail fall, Swift felt ready to dissipate into the sky with the unfettered wind.

Justus, following him around the ship to portside, was clapping.

Edric backed up from the rail and ducked beneath the sails to the stern, where he stayed.

Caius and Trystan threw down ropes.

Swift caught them and tied them to the *Strider's* gunwale, then dropped onto her bench.

The stint on the *Strider* had been exhilarating, but he was aching and grateful it was over. He'd just have to manage one sail, probably, while they all worked the *Regulus* together to sail north to the cove.

Justus leaned over the rail. "Brilliant work, lad. You should be proud."

Swift's smile could not be checked. "Can we sail north now? We've got plenty of light."

Justus, though smiling brightly, was shaking his head. "There are lessons still unfinished for you here. Climb up, and Caius will put you on the jib."

Swift's smile departed as he watched Justus disappear.

"Climb on," Caius called down.

Swift peeked around the hull of the big ship to glimpse his cove.

Its blue waves had grown even bluer with the sun, tending west.

Every rise of every wave looked like a beckoning hand.

"Swift," said Caius, one eyebrow raised.

"But—the treasure," said Swift, low enough that Justus might not hear.

Caius leaned on the rail. "Your best shot at treasure hunting involves cooperating."

Swift gathered the slack on the tow rope and drew the *Strider* to the *Regulus*. "I know how to sail, now. It's time we went after it."

Caius glanced over his shoulder, then lowered his voice further. "Some true practice at sailing is part of going after your treasure, right?"

Swift shrugged. "Yeah, but—"

"Many things, which you might pursue, are complicated like this," said Caius. "The path isn't always direct. Often, it involves a lot of work you might not've expected."

Swift climbed onto the netting tacked to the flank of the *Regulus*.

"Not everything you want will be right there in front of you," Caius kept on. "Not everything will be just a quick sail away. There's a lot of sweat involved. And to be good at it, you actually must love it."

Swift paused in his climb and watched Caius.

"Treating it like a passing interest isn't going to cut it." Caius straightened. "You have to learn to love the struggle itself, not just the win. And you can't expect immediate success. You have to get really, really good at standing back up after you've been punched down."

"What are you talking about?" asked Swift.

Caius reached down his hand. "Treasure hunting."

Swift climbed to the top of the netting and let Caius guide him over the rail.

8

*S*wift hung in for hours.

He'd listened as well as he could, performed as effectively as he could, stayed as responsive as possible to Justus' teaching, to Caius' corrections.

Finally, now, the sun was shining red and dipping its gossamer rays into the golden mist gathering in the west.

Swift had asked twice whether they could call the lesson done and take the *Regulus* north to Sterncastle Cove, to scout for the Star of Atlantis, as that was the point.

His first request had been answered by Edric arguing that it'd been Swift himself who'd begged for a sailing lesson, and that nothing on a ship could be learned quickly.

Swift's second request had been dismissed with a reminder from Justus that treasure wasn't the point. Respect for wind and water was.

Wind and water had certainly thrown their weight around, making every task a thousand times more difficult than doing it on land—more than half of Swift's tries at trimming sails had needed adjusting from Caius.

Swift's knots hadn't been very good since he reboarded the ship, but after a whole afternoon of standing his ground against wind, of struggling with ropes against the booms and bowsprit, of handling scratchy nylon and stiff canvas with damp, cold fingers, his knots were worthless.

His hands were chapped and bleeding in places, and he looked a wreck, he knew, his curly hair a blown-out mess, his red bruise throbbing beneath his father's sweater, singing out his moment of incompetence, and his legs had all but gone to rubber on the rocking deck, stumbling him like he'd been at the grog.

"*In fifty years of sailing free,*" Swift muttered, "*I never thought my eyes would see.*" He yanked a knotted line, but his grip slipped.

He let a cry and tripped back, staring at his hand, a ruddy rope burn crossing his palm.

He wiped his stinging skin, wet with sweat and spray, on his pajama bottoms, then again seized the rope.

"*The sun go red, the waves go warm – the clouds collide: the perfect storm.*"

The pirate shanty had been keeping him company all afternoon, giving him an outlet for his frustration and his ecstasy. He pictured his brothers getting stirred up by the shanty and joining in. Maybe asking to see his book or the map. Maybe nudging Justus in their influential way to get on with treasure hunting.

But no one had.

Trystan had noticed Swift looking at the map once, but he'd taken no interest in it. He'd only dropped an obvious, unhelpful reminder that treasure maps are known to carry the unfortunate side effect of summoning sea monsters.

Swift yanked the stubborn knot.

A hostile gale roared in and swept the rope from his hand.

Caius, who'd been watching him struggle for the past half hour, rose off the bench.

Swift snatched the rope and bellowed, "*Yo Ho, Yo Ho – Crack the boom and bend the crow! Yo Ho, Yo Ho – Over the swell we go.*"

Caius took the rope from Swift.

Relieved of it, Swift felt like dropping in a heap right there on the deck.

But that's not what someone who loved treasure and ships and seas and waves and wind would do. It isn't what someone who'd successfully sailed a dinghy way out west and brought her straight to portside would do.

Someone keen on sailing and salt gales and monsters and Celtic stars and pirate treasure would man a mast for sailing north.

"I think Justus will say you're done." Caius glanced toward the stern, where Justus was resting with the others.

Trystan and Edric had entirely left Swift to his exercises, just glancing at him from time to time, laughter on their faces.

Justus had been watching him not with an eye of criticism, nor with jest, but with what looked like appraisal. Even admiration.

Caius winked into the setting sun. "You've outlasted them, you know."

Justus came away from the stern, Edric and Trystan following.

"What a day you've given the *Regulus*." Justus' eyes, though fixed on Swift's, seemed distanced. "How hard you've worked. How much wind you've bridled."

Perhaps he was thinking back to the days when he was learning to sail—when he was responsive to the call to set off and seek ocean treasures.

"I must say," Justus went on, "I'm quite awed."

Swift pressed his hand to his pocketed book. "Are we sailing north for the cove now?"

"We're sailing for the dock," said Edric.

Swift held back. "We've got treasure still unhunted."

"We've also got wet clothes to dry and bellies to feed," said Trystan.

Justus held out his arm, to guide Swift to the stern. "You'll help me steer the ship to shore."

Swift glanced at Edric, standing by the foremast. "Can't I

at least mind a mast or something?" Helping was a deck boy's work. "I've been handling sails all day."

"Arguing all day is more like it," said Edric.

Swift tried to muster the presence of mind to spit a retort, but he was too beat to engage.

Justus steered him to the stern. "What's all this singing I've been hearing?"

"It's from *The Star of Atlantis*," said Swift. "That song might've been sung by pirates in the deeps of the North Atlantic."

Justus lifted his brow. "It could be that there still are pirates in the deeps of the North Atlantic."

"There is still one." Swift watched as Justus loosened the rudder. "My book says the Star of Atlantis is guarded by an undead pirate called Grog Blossom."

"Huh," said Justus. "Sounds ferocious."

Swift knelt to study how Justus was manipulating the rudder. The *Strider's* rudder was similar, and the two seemed to operate the same way.

"Can I have another go in the *Strider*?"

Justus trained Swift's hands to the rudder and guided him to steer. "Perhaps tomorrow."

"But I need more practice. I could sail her north—just to the mouth of that cove, to have a look in. It wouldn't take long."

Justus adjusted the rudder in Swift's hands. "You've worked harder today than many lads might. And your handling of the *Strider* was superb. That's to your credit. But it doesn't follow that you're ready to take her into close-reaching northerly winds and rocky terrains. Anyway, you'll soon be stiff as a rig and probably won't feel like it."

Swift kept his gaze on the cove. "Tomorrow, can we see about the treasure?"

Justus, measuring the clouds banking the horizon, didn't answer.

"Do you even care about the treasure?"

Justus brought his attention back to the rudder. "Yes, lad. We shall see."

When they neared the dock, Caius hauled the *Strider* close to the big ship and tied her there, rocking.

Swift watched her buck. "Kids do sail dinghies, up and down the coast, all the time. Ash has a dinghy of his very own. I know loads more about knots and booms and sails and rudders and lines than he does. Probably, I know more about sailing than all the kids who went out on the water today."

"That may be true." Justus stood to nestle the *Regulus* close to the dock. "But you're also more roughly worked. It'd be foolish to test the sea today more than you have."

"Test the sea..."

There'd been a stupid misstep, which was small potatoes and resulted in nothing more than a tiny bruise on a rib. Then he'd handled the dinghy like a pro, though for just a short distance.

The truth was, he'd been static on the *Regulus*, nearly all day, fussing with her lines. He'd hardly ridden the sea, much less tested it.

He went to the berth and knelt before the trapdoor. He tried to take his duffle bag from Trystan, coming up the ladder from below, but Trystan kept it.

"I can manage it for you," said Trystan.

Swift pulled it off him and shouldered the strap. "I'll manage it."

"The campsite's a good quarter mile from here. If you need help, ask."

Swift pushed past him. "I can manage it."

9

Swift watched Justus build a campfire while the brothers laid out bedrolls.

Their campsite, on the brink of the Wentletrap Forest, seemed like an island between two magnificent seas—one an indigo chorus of gamboling waves, the other oaken and silent as death.

Swift tried to listen to the talk and throw in a bit every now and then, but his face was tingly with salt and sunburn, and he could hardly hold himself upright.

His father and brothers had been on the sea all day, just the same as he had, beneath the same beating sun and cold wind, breathing the same salt-mist, on the same rocking waves—yet they still looked alive. Whatever second wind they caught seemed to have blown right by him.

If he was made of ships and sails, if he was a high-born treasure hunter, he felt a failure to his heritage. He'd gotten nowhere close to the Star of Atlantis.

He kicked his way beneath the covers.

Justus, though—still watching him—had seemed pleased with Swift's effort.

He'd said—"What a day you've given the *Regulus*." "How

hard you've worked." "How much wind you bridled." "I must say—I'm quite awed."

Regardless, Swift hadn't managed to go venturing, even with a ship at his disposal, and a crew, and skills, and everything.

Right this minute, he might be within shouting distance of the Star of Atlantis—and yet all his attempts to reach it had fizzled.

If Justus was so awed, he should've recognized that Swift deserved more chances on the *Strider*. At the very least, he deserved a glimpse inside that cove.

Swift opened his book's plastic bag and peeped at his map by firelight.

The painted star seemed smaller in the dark. Washed out.

Maybe someone else had found the treasure today, and maybe this was a magical map, and maybe the Celtic star marked here would vanish if the treasure were lifted from the sea.

He tucked away his book and lay back. If the treasure were taken, Edric would make sure Swift felt the pain of it.

Swift listened to the droning campfire talk as silver clouds quickened past the rising moon and crossed the navy sky like airborne galley ships, catching the North Atlantic's flashing on their hulls. Little stars shivered alight like sardines driven to the skim.

Swift took in the sea-freshened air, tinged handsome with pine resin. He watched the last pale streak of twilight's glow evaporate from the western canopy as his heavy lids fell closed.

"The lad did well today," said Justus.

Swift's eyes popped open.

He lay rigid, and set to breathing deeply, like in sleep.

"He did seem to gain a stronger grasp on his capabilities," said Trystan. "Maybe you'll have luck—"

"This isn't about Swift's capabilities," said Edric. "What the lad needs is control."

"He's getting there," said Caius.

"He still doesn't know how to measure his temper," said Edric.

"How long will he think that complaining and begging will get him where he wants to go?" Edric flicked an ember-tipped stick into the fire.

Swift bit his lips.

"It was you who aggravated that temper," said Caius.

"I had nothing to do with it." Edric held out his hands, warming them over the fire. "The lad can be so bullheaded, especially when things aren't going his way."

"That determination's been there all his life." Justus focused on Edric. "And it does remind me of someone." He glanced at each of the others. "Now confess, did we not, today, witness Swift's competence gleaming?"

Truth be told, even having failed at pursuing the treasure, Swift had felt an elation of competence. Sailing today had made him feel somehow older.

"Together with his intellect, Swift's determination betrays fierce potential," said Justus. "He could do anything he likes, once that's channeled; once he realizes how far his capabilities might take him."

As thrilling as it was to hear those words from his father, they weren't true.

Justus didn't want Swift to do "anything he liked." He was clearly thinking only of the Practicum.

Treasure chasing, Swift certainly felt born to. But could he reasonably consider himself capable enough to chase something as difficult as medicine?

Testing into that Practicum would certainly be a challenge demanding competence—though of a very different kind than he'd ever faced.

"I must say—I'm quite awed," Swift whispered to himself.

"It wasn't all that long ago that Swift would answer to nothing but 'Captain Corkscrew,'" said Edric.

The fire spat with him spearing its heart with a stick.

"He's shown us today that he's still that same lad."

Swift's own heart seared at that.

Because Edric was right.

Justus probably didn't have four sons who could awe him as they conquered real challenges.

Rather, he likely had three sons and a lad.

"Swift's as playful as any lad ought to be," said Caius. "But his intellect is far beyond his years. That has to impress even you."

"Okay, so he's a ninny," said Edric, laughter in his voice. "That doesn't promise he'll amount to anything."

Swift felt the cool of Caius' shadow, passing between him and the fire.

"Don't be like that," said Edric. "We're just having a spirited debate."

Swift turned his head the merest bit to see Caius, through a veil of juniper woodsmoke, digging into the cooler.

Caius closed the cooler and sat on its lid, well away from Edric. He handed Trystan a bottle.

"Swift's untried." Trystan uncapped the beer. "I think Father's right, though. If Swift can just realize the magnitude of his capabilities, success will no doubt breed success."

"And this is the material point," said Justus. "He's highly driven when it comes to sea legends. Just imagine, he'd be a force to be reckoned with, were he to gather a vision of—"

"You're dead right that the lad needs to catch fire." Edric leaned back against a tree. "Swift needs to do something outrageous and marvelous—he's got to get addicted to the feeling of joy, of conquest."

Caius tossed Edric a beer.

"But the question is"—Edric caught it and cracked off its lid—"will he ever have the command, the self-confidence, to manage it?"

Swift shrouded himself more with the blanket, so no one might see the unmanageable smile spreading across his face.

He'd never heard his brothers and Justus all together discussing him like this. And they were mostly dropping words of their belief in him—now, even Edric was.

So what if those words were veiled with the criticism of

his being untried and childish? Edric had used the words "Swift" and "conquest" in the same sentence.

"Sailing's a beastly sport," said Trystan. "Learning the ropes, it feels like every bloody thing's against you. Remember what a tosser Edric was at this stage? The only reason he got through lessons was because Father had him convinced that sailing skills apply to other, more delicate fields."

A bit of shuffling ended in Trystan getting shoved off the log and landing by Swift's feet.

Swift managed not to move. The brothers all were laughing. So was Justus.

"Swift needs the chance to confront new challenges," said Justus. "If he takes them on, I've no doubt he'll—as Edric says—catch fire."

"And he needs to go at those challenges without being criticized." Caius glanced at Edric. "Or sabotaged."

10

Swift slept soundly until the wind picked up in the wee hours. When he opened his eyes, the stations of the silver stars told him it was just after midnight.

He twisted onto his side and watched a mist drift north, from the west, and vanish among the high, twisting trees edging the Wentletrap Forest. The rhythm of distant water splashing the shoreline changed tempo with the shifting of the winds. All the men were snoring.

He snuck out his flashlight and snuggled beneath his covers. He pulled his book from its plastic bag and thumbed through its pages, admiring how artistically scribed were the navigation tactics and records of weather. He stopped when he reached the spread of water monsters, and beside it, the small section describing the path to the treasure:

When the shore draws long and straight, skim the briny banks. Be swallowed by Sterncastle Cove. Seek the islet, round as Earth, studded with Kraken fangs. Mind the deeps for mermaid tails, shimmering blue and green. Heed their song, but touch the water not, lest your life be forfeit to their goddess. Always keep a weather eye on the mist coiling in the cove, for through it

*paddles old Grog Blossom, always dead, yet ever awake, cursed
to forever sail as watchman over the Star of Atlantis.*

On the facing page was drawn the silver star, crowning a
chest nestled inside a tumble of sharply squared rocks—actual
Kraken teeth, by the looks of them—driven hard into the
seabed.

"*In fifty years of sailing free, I never thought my eyes
would see,*" Swift whispered.

The Star of Atlantis must be precious indeed to lie within
a cove guarded by murderous mermaids and an undead
pirate.

"*The sun go red, the waves go warm, the clouds collide –
the perfect storm.*"

Swift flipped to the page where the oath lay. He reread it
solemnly, then turned pages to the pirate song and whispered
it to the cadence of the far-off breakers.

The singing set a hunger in his bones to feel the sea.

He sat up, his mind amok with monsters.

In the broad light of day, it was easy to cast off as ridicu-
lous the stories of mythical sea beasts. In the black of night,
however, with this crying wind and with the coast shivering in
hungry crashes of waves, believing them was easy.

Lying still, listening to the wind on the water, Swift could
understand why some sailors actually did.

In the face of all those monsters, how brave, how competent, how determined must the sailor in this verse have been
to stay the rig and charge the deck and hoist the sails and
strike the bloody colors down alone?

In the verse, there was no able crew. It was just one pirate
holding off the power of the storming sea.

The itch to touch sails and ropes ignited in Swift's fingers.

He pressed the sore place on his chest where the boom
had struck him. It barely smarted.

Justus had predicted he'd be stiff as a rig—but he wasn't.
Maybe he'd done so well at sailing as to bypass the weakness
of body that most novice sailors faced.

In that moment of striking water, of plummeting down, airless, what might he have done if Caius and Justus hadn't been there?

Would he have been able to right himself and climb back into the dinghy? Maybe. Probably.

Swift's limbs felt muscular and strong as bowsprits. If he'd tipped off the *Star Strider* without anyone around, he'd probably have gained his bearings quick.

He was a good swimmer and could've powered to the skim; could certainly have managed to swim back to the *Strider* and climb to safety.

Swift eased out of his bedroll. He slunk to the fire and warmed his hands over the dreaming embers. He studied each sleeping face around him.

Caius had said all Swift needed was a chance to go at challenges without criticism. Without Edric's jabs at sabotage.

That was exactly what he needed.

And Justus had said that Swift needed to try his hand at new challenges—that, in discovering for himself his true competence, he might catch fire.

Those had been Edric's words too.

But Edric had also called Swift a lad and a ninny; bull-headed. He'd always been impatient with Swift; he'd always seemed to see Swift as someone who wouldn't amount to much.

But what did Edric know? Justus had let Swift pilot the *Strider* solo, even after the buck. And he'd spoken so strongly of how well Swift had done. They all had.

There was only one thing Justus had said Swift wasn't ready for: sailing the dinghy through rougher terrain, which was hogwash. It was a complete contradiction to his diagnosis that Swift needed a chance to go after new challenges.

Justus clearly wanted to withhold that particular, delicious chance—that reward—until Swift had paid his dues with technique; to make him trim a thousand sails before granting him the gratification of commanding the *Star Strider* north to Sterncastle Cove.

How ecstatic would be the sensation of all that lively water lifting him, carrying him through the starlit sea to hidden treasure?

The cool salt wind picked up, brushing Swift's cheeks and stirring the corkscrew curls out of his eyes—it felt like the hands of a sea goddess, coaxing him west.

Swift unfolded the map all the way.

He angled it to let the firelight strike its inked shores and liven its waves.

The coast was so well-drawn that the more prominent landmarks were detailed, if not recognizable. As were the large clusters of rocks and coves. The flickering flames seemed to cast shadows upon the odd markings, almost giving them dimensionality.

Swift looked more closely at them.

Might firelight reveal those strange pen strokes as letters that he could actually read?

He lifted the map until he could see the bright embers dancing through the parchment as behind an antique hearth screen.

The lettering remained unreadable. Cryptic.

What remained plain, however, was the drawing of the coast.

The shoreline just to the north of their camp was shaped so much like this. Sterncastle Cove, it really might be.

So, here was an excellent challenge. He could sail the *Strider* and make it to Sterncastle Cove alone, just like the pirate in his book had.

But. What if there were monsters in the water?

Swift raised his head, letting the cold tendrils of wind caress him as he studied the shore.

The distant sloshing of the sea was soft, and in it he couldn't help but pick up on what might be tentacles slapping waves. Or perhaps sheets of water draining off a huge, gnarled head, rising to frisk the shore with glowing eyes. Or maybe the crippled gait of an undead pirate.

He gazed at the map, flickering with the fire's dance.

Trystan was right when he'd mentioned that treasure maps are known, in lore, to beckon sea creatures. What if that was based on something real?

If legendary sea beasts trolled these waters, they might've been watching him all day—might've been hearing him sing of the Star of Atlantis. They might be lurking now, in those shallows, just beyond the camp.

That thought alone made his heart jump to a quicker clip.

He'd sighted nothing wicked in the water, though, neither legendary nor common—not a shark, not a mermaid's tail, not a tentacle, not a fin. Not once in the whole day.

But. Sharks and monsters might more often hunt by night than day. Every book on sea monsters he'd read had said as much.

Swift looked toward the sea, adrenaline pumping in him hard.

He'd braved those Celtic waters all through the sunny day, and that was something. So in this night, now, might he brave its monsters?

How could he call himself "competent" on any score if he weren't capable of trying?

He lay the map on the sandy earth and studied the way into Sterncastle Cove.

He'd seen the pass through the rocks from the deck of the *Regulus*, and the course was quite clear. It wasn't even very far.

But. Considering the volume of monsters in the pirate verse, it seemed foolish to try for the treasure without the support of an able-bodied crew.

But. The pirate in the verse had done it solo. A crew, to sea monsters, might seem a threat. One sailor alone, they might not regard.

If he could manage to pilot the *Strider* into Sterncastle Cove and glimpse the treasure, confirming that the map was trustworthy—if he could just make it there and back to camp before sunrise, not only would he have impressive things to say about the sea at night, but he'd also have amazing things to tell about its monsters.

And he'd have laid eyes on the Star of Atlantis.

At his report, Justus and the brothers would jump to set off and see what Swift had seen.

And Swift himself could navigate because he'd been up the coast and back.

This was his chance to ride the *Strider* north, completely on his own, like Caius had said.

He'd show himself a real-deal treasure hunter, great of determination, fulfilling what Justus saw in him, and creating a proof of where Swift ought to be.

There couldn't be a better way to experience true competence.

This is how he might catch fire.

Swift tied on his shoes, almost dry from resting fireside.

He slipped on his waterproof under suit, toasty warm.

He threaded on his trousers and windbreaker and started to slip his father's warm sweater over them, but—

No legitimate sailor, nor pirate, would go around in his father's sweater.

Unless that father were dead, and he'd plundered it off his cold body.

But Justus was looking lively, snoring up a storm beside the fire.

Swift tossed the sweater away, over his empty bedroll.

He slipped his book and map, carefully sealed, into the pocket of his trousers.

He eased Caius' bandana from alongside his pillow.

Caius stretched his arm.

Swift froze.

If he were caught leaving, this would be difficult to explain. His plan would really only make sense to them once he'd come back, tested and successful, bearing stories, the *Strider* docked masterfully and sleeping happy in a strip of water visible from camp.

Swift slipped away from Caius; watched his eyes to see if they'd stay sealed.

Caius didn't move again. His breathing remained deep and even.

Swift glanced at their father.

If Justus opened his eyes, he'd bustle up, stuff Swift right back in his bedroll, and tie his ankle to Caius. It wouldn't be the first time.

When he was certain everyone would stay dead asleep, Swift snuck away from the camp.

Once clear of the firelight, he charged the coast.

11

Swift stood on the cold beach, arrow straight and empty for miles, inside a darkness seeming thick enough to be taken by the handfuls.

Into this abyss he'd go alone—a challenge, yes, and a step through the misty door of master seamanship and maritime treasure hunting.

He checked the stars.

There was Leo, roaring overhead and westward, marking the dawn at three hours off.

When he returned, he'd quietly stoke the fire and get the coffee going.

He'd sit in his father's camping chair, poking the embers with a stick, stirring the coffee from time to time, dipping Justus' blue tin cup into it and sipping at the scalding, bitter brew, not bothering, the way Justus and the others never bothered, that he was burning his hands and mouth with the awful stuff.

Caius, Trystan, and Edric would rouse and see him wide awake, tending everything, and he'd nonchalantly say that he'd been up the coast and back.

That he'd scouted out the Star of Atlantis treasure, and wasn't it a fine morning?

Sip.

Justus would stand over him, rubbing his beard as he asked, *"How'd you manage to do it, Swift? Sail the Strider at night—when monsters are known to roam? (He'd shake his head.) Why, we, none of us, have ever tried any challenge so bold."*

And it would be "Swift," not "lad," because he'd been up the coast and back. In the *Strider*. On his own.

Swift glanced over his shoulder to where their camp lay, nestled within a thicket of juniper trees.

The plot was silent as a grave. He couldn't even see the dying fire.

He scuttled along the waterline to the dock.

The sea to the west shimmered beneath a watery moon and a dense display of stars. It looked like a hundred-million galleon coins were floating on the waves.

In the distance, the *Regulus* slept, unmoved by the skittery sea.

The dinghy was pale, its hull a smile on the water. Tripping gleefully over every surge, she looked as wide awake as Swift felt.

She seemed to be waiting for him.

Swift quickened and turned down the dock in a full run. He caught himself on a docking post and halted before the *Star Strider*.

The water in the west, its surface a touch warm this deep in summer, carried a mist that was rolling in over the skim, in billowy clouds.

A drive of wind pushed back the tendrils of fog, unveiling the distant North Atlantic as a squidy, inkpot black.

Swift studied his dark silhouette rippling in the water off the dock.

Wild-haired and bony, he looked every bit as hard and sinewy as a real-deal pirate. Every bit as competent.

Up rose thrilling memories of the swashbuckler fantasies he and Ash used to create.

He pulled out Caius' bandana and wrapped it around his head, drawing up every corkscrew coming off him.

"I be Captain Corkscrew, Pirate Prince of the Western Shires," Swift told the dinghy. "And ye be me beauty, the dauntless *Star Strider*, and ye shall carry me to hidden treasure."

The dinghy looked impressed. She seemed to bare her teeth a touch, giving a good and hearty pirate growl as the sea bucked up her hull.

Swift climbed aboard and strapped on his life jacket. There were no brothers to see to his sure footing, so he minded every precaution.

Being alone at this made him more accountable. This was definitely the best way to take on new challenges.

Justus, if he could see what Swift was up to, would admire how careful and deliberate were each of Swift's decisions, his every placement of hand and foot calculated. Resolute.

The *Strider* was knotted to the *Regulus*, but Swift made quick work of freeing her.

He cranked on the *Strider's* light, then settled his foot upon the bow, asserting his balance and keeping a strong grip on the mast.

"Ahoy me hearties!" Swift proclaimed, the dinghy swelling in his mind to vast proportions, its every nook and cranny growing peopled with bilge-sucking pirates.

"Avast Ye! We be after the Star of Atlantis this black morn. Look alive ye salty scum. Weigh the anchor and hoist the mizzen. We be off!"

Swift tugged the line and flared the sail.

The wind cooperated, blowing the canvas broad and carrying Swift seaward.

"I don't take kindly to the prospect of Sterncastle Cove this misty morn," growled Mister Hogwash, Swift's worst pirate.

"Ye be squiffy Mister Hogwash. Swab the deck, or I'll have you strung to dance Jack Ketch."

"It be looking like a red and stormy dawn awaits," said

Mister Hogwash, leaning on his mop, peering at the black east. "I'd bet me last tooth we'll be sunk."

Swift switched to sitting at the ship's stern. "That be jolly nonsense. Get below and swab the brig."

"There be fearsome monsters in the water," said old, bent Mister Hogwash, winking one old eye. "Ye be a bullheaded ninny to seek the dread Atlantis Star."

A simmering chatter rumbled from the other seadogs.

Nobody—absolutely nobody—disrespected Captain Corkscrew.

Mister Hogwash threw down his mop. "A ship of fools, this be. Hang young Corkscrew and be done! I be taking charge of this *Star Strider*."

Swift advanced on the old salt. "How are ye going to do that"—he swiped his cutlass from his belt—"if you're dead?"

"Fool of a captain," spat Mister Hogwash, crooking beneath the whetted shank. "You'll sail us all straight to our sunken graves."

Captain Corkscrew brandished his blade. "Cleave him to the Brisket!"

The pirate crew fell fast on Mister Hogwash, knotting the arms and legs of the mutineer with ropes and lashing him to the hull, portside.

With Mister Hogwash subdued, Swift had a moment to look about him.

The *Strider* was moving at a lively clip. The wind was high and steady, like the first breath of a storm, and a snappy longshore current was pulling him due north.

Though the wind was indeed gustier than the draw that'd pulled him west, it was nothing he couldn't handle. And though the waves looked rougher, rockier, near the cove, balancing the *Strider* was something he'd always been good at. And he'd done really well at keeping her pitch and roll in check all through his practice run.

Justus' words seemed to ring true. Swift could handle new challenges. And when he had the Star of Atlantis in hand, Justus and everyone would realize Swift's destiny.

Swift fixed the mainsail with a mezzo-slackness that nicely caught the gale and quickened his clip.

The thought of deep blue northern waters and crisp northerly winds slipped into him, keeping his joints nimble and his sore fingers effective at manipulating knots.

Although—his father's prediction of rigid muscles was turning out to have some truth.

The pirates, every bit as raw as Swift, stirred up a shanty. Swift rallied with them and sang:

IN FIFTY YEARS of sailing free –
I never thought my eyes would see
the sun go red, the waves go warm –
the clouds collide: the perfect storm.
Yo Ho, Yo Ho – Crack the boom and bend the crow!
Yo Ho, Yo Ho – Over the swell we go.

THE WIND PICKED up and filled the sail. Swift fed more slack and charged the sharpening waves.

THE MEN ALL DRUNK, locked in the brig,
I drain the grog and stay the rig!
The men asleep, the sea in rage,
the kraken creeps from out its cage.
Yo Ho, Yo Ho – Flair the jib and jet the bow!
Yo Ho, Yo Ho – Into the waves we blow.

SWIFT FINISHED the verse as the first tendrils of dawn unfurled shafts of steely gray across the east.

Full dawn was still far off, but the sea and coast, though quite dark, were turning visible.

A boy who sailed by night and safely returned before anyone knew anything was one thing. But a boy found missing from his bunk and nowhere—with a dinghy gone—was quite another.

Swift checked the sea behind him.

He startled when his gaze fell upon the *Regulus*, docked in the near distance to the south.

He felt sure he'd traveled further from her than this, what with the heaving waves and gusty wind.

Scanning the shoreline, he startled again as small figures manifested on the beach. They were pointing at him.

Swift examined his options.

Sailing straight for shore, straight to them, was an option, though a poor one. If he did that, he'd be the one dancing Jack Ketch. But perhaps Justus would be less mad if he could watch Swift sail in, dinghy intact and upright.

A push of mist washed over the waves, obscuring the shore and immersing Swift.

The mist was metal cold, like a poisonous vapor breathed from the abode of a kraken—the kind of mist, it seemed, that undead pirates would troll.

On the back of that mist, a second option drifted to Swift. It was as though the sea itself, or maybe the *Strider*, or maybe the crew of buccaneers, were whispering a plan.

A smile crept across Swift's face. It was a very good plan.

If he were to break for land beyond Sterncastle Cove...if he were to reach the coast, just a bit further north...he could run ashore near their beach house. If he could make it there, he'd outrun his father's anger.

Justus surely would feel proud of him for sailing all that way. And he'd be found settled on the sofa, safe with Mum.

What could Justus say?

A strip of wind parted the mist and showed the figures on the coast, waving arms.

"Sail ho!" cried Swift. "We be sighted!"

The bilge-sucking buccaneers were all drunk, fast asleep.

"All hands on deck!" Swift went around the little ship, kicking his pirates to life. "Peabrain, man the chase gun! Jolly

Stormcrow, take the wheel!" Swift set the rudder true to north and rolled the knot along the boom, flaring the mainsail broad.

The men on the coast read the open sail and broke their line, sprinting for the *Regulus*.

The *Strider*, catching full wind, set into a sprint across the waves.

A racing stallion breaking free its gate could not have been more spirited.

"The *Strider* be a clipper now!" Swift laughed his heartiest laugh. "Set the course for Brandy Brook and make ye fast the jib. Or ready your biscuits for Captain Justus' flog!"

Swift got right on making fast the jib, and the *Strider* responded true, jumping wave after wave, tearing north.

"Peabrain, mind the halyard! Jolly Stormcrow, take us in! A Kraken's nest lies true to north, and there be treasure stowed."

Swift glanced over the gunwale and found Mister Hogwash's ropes had come untied. "If ye be undone, Mister Hogwash, look alive and mind the jib. The *Regulus* is gaining in our wake."

A noise...a low noise, like dark laughter, sounded.

Swift let the rope go slack.

He peered seaward, through the mist.

In the western expanse, deep within the swirling gray mist, floated a long boat—a skiff with one bare mast.

No light shone from the skiff. Her form was etched by just the moon and stars, making her a gray hole on the otherwise black water. The skiff was quite far behind him, but close enough for Swift to hear that oars were plunking in the water.

Oars worked by a single, shadowed figure.

12

*A*t the sound of that skiff, gliding closer, the line slipped from Swift's hands.

The *Strider's* mainsail fluttered slack. Waves rolled beneath the dinghy, offsetting her yaw.

Swift clung to the mast, his breathing quickening beyond what he could control.

He recognized the reaching feeling in his lungs as panic.

It'd been a while since an attack had set in, and he'd never had a one without Caius or Mum near.

The darkness felt like a blanket pressing his face.

He clutched at the knots on the sail. He tried to slow his mind. Forced his diaphragm to take air. Focused on the easing sail.

All his eyes would look at, though, was the gray wedge the skiff was cutting from the pattern of choppy waters.

The skiff looked like a common fishing boat—but why would any fisherman be out at night without a light?

He tried to make out whether the person in the boat was watching him. Whether the skiff really was easing his way.

A whistling wheedled through the mist.

It was a dead-breathed whistling, drawing the melody of the verse in *The Star of Atlantis*.

The pirate-ghost sentry to the treasure would certainly know its song.

Grog Blossom.

Swift heaved his weight onto the block. He jerked the line tight and did everything to widen the mast.

A wave washed the *Strider*, shoving her off kilter.

Swift nearly tumbled over the gunwale, but he grabbed the mast and leaned in, tipping her left and right until the *Strider* and he together mastered their balance.

A cramp started under his shoulder blade and spread into his neck. It arched his back and pinched his breath.

He gripped the mast as waves sloshed over the *Strider's* side, threatening to swamp her.

The cramp diminished enough for Swift to snatch the rudder with his working arm. He steadied the boat against the waves until she was fully upright, wind fluttering her wild sail.

The cramp released him, its easing feeling like tentacles slipping away.

With its going, the panic lessened.

Swift sat upright and looked back at the skiff.

It hadn't moved.

Its rider was holding an oar flat across the boat's breadth.

Though the skiff was a good distance off, it was pointed straight at him.

Swift scooted to the block and trimmed the sail until it again caught the wind.

The skiff moved when he did, its long oar rising, then dipping. Rising, then dipping. With each stroke, the skiff seemed to gain a meter on him.

Swift peered ahead and sighted the sheltered divot in the water.

It seemed, in every way, to be Sterncastle Cove. The Kraken-tooth rocks in its center that would give it away were concealed by the mist, but the coast had truly been stick straight leading up to this.

Maybe the Star of Atlantis was wanting to be found.

It was said to choose its discoverer. Maybe it was sending currents to draw him true, safe from dread Grog Blossom.

If that was Grog Blossom.

Pirate fantasies were well enough, but even if rooted in some truth, they were fantasies. And here he was, alone in a sailing dinghy, being stalked by an absolute stranger.

What could anyone possibly want with a boy alone on the North Atlantic, at night, though?

Probably nothing. If that were a regular fisherman, he'd likely just leave Swift alone.

But if that were a regular fisherman, what were the chances that he'd know that shanty?

And why was he closing in?

And why didn't he have a light?

A glance over his shoulder showed the *Regulus* taking to sea.

His family probably couldn't see the skiff, dark as she was on the water, quite far ahead of their hull.

The *Regulus* had not just sails, but an engine and could reach him in minutes.

Swift watched her, listening for an ignition.

The sails broadened, but the engine didn't fire.

If the *Regulus* caught him, it would mean a world of hurt.

But the thought of his father's furious face felt mild compared to the visions rising of the man in the skiff snatching him.

Whether that sailor was dread Grog Blossom or some loony seaman, he might really have a blade. He might really carry a gun.

A madman could make quick work of slicing Swift's throat or lodging a bullet in him, claiming the *Strider,* and speeding off into the black. Swift's body would drift out to sea before anyone on the *Regulus* could be the wiser.

Swift's constricting chest prickled with the thought of that sailor holding a knife.

He slackened the *Strider's* sails and focused on the *Regulus*, willing her to quicken and flank herself between him and the weird skiff.

Her pace seemed no more than a crawl.

And the skiff was advancing. Fast.

Swift couldn't wait for the *Regulus*. He had to do something.

He spread his mainsail as wide as it would go. But even sailing at its quickest clip, the *Strider* had no chance of making it to the beach house before the skiff caught up.

Swift looked ahead, assessing the graying coast.

The entrance to Sterncastle Cove was narrow. Perhaps too narrow for a skiff. Certainly, too narrow for a brigantine.

But it was perfect for the *Strider*.

If he could reach that islet of Kraken teeth, maybe he'd find the treasure resting there in plain sight. If that were Grog Blossom on his tail—and if Swift actually managed to reach the Star of Atlantis—maybe at the finding of the treasure, the undead buccaneer would be undone.

And if that wasn't Grog Blossom, if it were some creepy seadog really stalking him, the cove seemed Swift's only refuge.

If he could make it there, his family would see him go in. And if the skiff followed, they'd see that, too. They'd charge the engine and call for help.

Swift glanced over his shoulder to find the sails of the *Regulus* falling slack.

Were they prepping the engine, then?

But the great ship stayed quiet.

The only sound on the water was the slip of oars rising and falling. Rising and falling.

The skiff was still a good distance behind him, but its creep felt like the raising of a blade.

Swift kept his eyes fixed on the passage into the cove. If he were lucky, he'd glide right in. If he were not lucky, he'd tip into an eddy along the gateway.

A current snagged the *Strider* and shot it toward the pass. Breakers splashed the dinghy's starboard side, soaking Swift.

He threw his weight to counter the slosh.

Quick waves swept the *Strider* toward the mouth of Sterncastle Cove.

Swift gripped the mast and winced.

The *Strider's* fate was fully out of his hands.

13

Teetering on the top of a wave, at the brink of Sterncastle Cove—

it was like hanging in Titan's balance—the wave a scale that weighed Swift's heart against his deeds to judge if he were fit to live or die.

The wave let go of him.

In a rush of white froth, Swift slid between the rocks.

Clutching his chest, he sank off the bench. The *Strider* still cradled him, but that plunge down through steep waves into the cove—it struck as the same feeling as what arrested him earlier, at the *Strider's* buck—the sea swallowing him.

He crooked in the bowl until he had ahold of his breathing.

When the sense of wooziness faded, he sat up and took inventory of his ship.

The *Strider* was upright, surging on with the force of a strong current into the broad cove. Her sails were empty, but untorn.

High rocks drew a ring around him, casting shadows. The waves here were calm, almost flat, beneath the dense mist. The cove was void of wind.

Swift righted himself on the bench and studied the pass behind him.

He listened for any splashing—for waves striking a skiff's hull, for oars sweeping the sea.

Minutes crept of his rapid breathing, of wind shuddering the sails, of his heart skipping.

No splash of water struck a skiff, and no voice sounded. No pirate shanty lifted behind him. He heard nothing on the water but water.

Maybe the madman in the skiff had judged the pass too small, too difficult, and moved off.

Swift unfixed his oar.

Keeping an eye out for surfacing reefs, he swept the sea, easing the *Strider* through the mist, further into the cove.

The cove, with its rocky walls looming and heavy mists curling, carried an unearthly quality. It was as though in the mist hung not just the smell of fish and sea minerals, but magic.

Swift strained to make out anything that might be the Kraken-tooth islet—the islet that Sterncastle Cove ought to have in its center. He could shelter there; hide, until he was sure he was unfollowed.

The further he pulled in, though, the emptier he found the cove to be.

But its emptiness seemed suspect. It was as though a presence lingered here. Trespassing these still waters felt like slipping into a room that held somebody hiding.

Mermaids played along the Celtic coast at sunrise, sailors claimed.

Swift glanced down into the water.

Maybe a mermaid shoal was gliding underneath the *Strider*, at this moment—coasting closer. Maybe a shark had spotted his light and was nearing.

Gripping the oar, his heart in his throat, he peered over the gunwale.

Deep inside the translucent-gray water, right beneath the *Strider*, something swayed.

Swift abandoned the oar in his lap. He seized the *Strider's* edge with both hands.

The something in the water shifted from a shimmer to a swelling light. It glistened, brightened to a brilliant, electric blue.

The water seemed several fathoms deep right here—well deep enough for bigger sharks to coast. And surely it was deep enough for mermaids.

Swift glanced behind him.

The passage to Sterncastle Cove still stood vacant.

Maybe the skiff's rider was looming—just beyond the rocks framing the entrance to the cove—waiting for Swift to sail back.

Or maybe, if that had been Grog Blossom, he'd plunged into the sea to suffer a second death.

Swift peered again into the water.

There, the bright something still slithered.

Flickered.

It was smaller than a shark would be. And sharks didn't shimmer like that.

If a mermaid sensed seawater coursing in Swift's blood, she'd rise and whisper ocean riddles. She'd fix her aqua eyes on his, mesmerizing him with her beauty.

And she'd vent melodies hauled from the open ocean— perhaps from the same place his pirate verse had been harvested.

Places of sunsetted seascapes where songs of the Celtic elements—songs of moons and starry skies, of forests and spirits and winds and enchantment—shanties of longing for silver and jewels, galleons and crowns—drifted in wait for a born treasure hunter to hear them.

Swift wrapped his fingers around the book, in his pocket.

The Star of Atlantis told of monsters unfathomable in these waters. Anything could be down there. Anything could be coming.

Water splashed from near the pass.

Swift jumped and spun.

The nose of the skiff threaded between the rocks.

The pass looked hardly wide enough for its sides to fit, but a second—and it was through.

The figure in the skiff's middle—close now and closing in—loomed featureless.

The figure's empty blackness seemed unnatural. Maybe the vacuity was just an effect of the deep shadows cast by the high rocks lining the cove. Or maybe it was a hellish dimness; an undead body stitched of shadows.

Swift's sore arms responded to the panic in his heart. He oared the *Strider* quickly away, straight to the middle of the cove, where the mist loomed thickest.

The islet ring of Kraken teeth should be right there.

Swift glided straight through the center of the cove with not so much as a reef tip to dodge.

There were no kraken teeth. There was no circlet of jetting rocks as round as Earth. There was nothing at all. This cove was like the sinkhole of a dead volcano—vast and void.

Swift squared the nose of the *Strider* at the skiff.

It was moving briskly on the placid water, the foul whistling of its occupant piercing the dank wind.

The dark water stayed an eerie calm as the glowing something in the depths ascended.

Perhaps whistling was how Grog Blossom summoned sentry mermaids.

A shock of thought froze Swift, arresting his oar and stopping his breath—

What if the skiff's rider hadn't discovered him here, but had driven him here? What if the map was actually a trap? What if its cryptic letters spelled out some kind of warning?

Maybe there was no Star of Atlantis.

Maybe the map had been drawn so sailors would come searching, so sailors would find what looked exactly like Sterncastle Cove—just as he had—that their bodies might be forfeit for anything to feast upon—Kraken, undead pirate, or mermaid goddess.

In a flash of gray, the water between the *Strider* and the skiff broke with a silver fin.

Swift gripped the mast and watched a blue-white body muscle out of the sea.

It leapt into the air—a ten-foot thrasher shark.

It arced and twisted. Its mouth gaped, showing teeth. It plunged down close enough to splash Swift's face.

His heart stuttering, Swift sank to the base of the *Strider*.

He'd been on the bow of the *Regulus*, a few summers back, when he'd seen a thrasher leap, just like that. Caius saw it too and told him thrashers jump to disturb the water; to stun fishes at the surface for catching and eating.

That leap meant the thrasher was hungry.

Hunting.

Swift sat confounded, too full of fear to even breathe, his back tingling with the sense of the shark beneath, perhaps rising to knock the *Strider* with its snout.

He'd read someplace that sharks could sense not just blood in the water, but blood inside a human body, in a boat— warm meat waiting to be shucked and eaten like a muscle in a cockle.

And bigger sharks were fully capable of tipping little boats.

He had to get out of the water.

Swift peered over the gunwale at the sloshing the shark left.

He lifted his gaze to the narrow pass and tried to calculate whether he had room to skate past the skiff.

The gap on either side of it was narrow, and the skiff's rider was keeping it that way, angling, it seemed, to block him.

And even if Swift could get by, what would that seadog do?

He'd followed Swift here. Chased him into a cove haunted by sharks and who knew what else? He'd certainly not let him pass.

Swift watched the water for signs that the shark was

circling back. But after a moment, the cove grew dead still again.

He couldn't even make out the footprint on the skim where the thrasher had landed.

The rock walls of the cove encroached. The mist constricted. The light in the deeps strengthened. The shark beneath him grew hungrier. The ragged figure drew nearer.

Swift hesitated to put his oar in the water with that shark, with that eerie blue glow—but he'd have to. The shoulders of these looming walls deflected any wind that could fill the *Strider's* sails. To get anywhere, he'd have to paddle.

Swift's arms felt weak, and his back was stiff and seemed on the verge of cramping again. Even if he could manage to steadily oar, the *Strider* would only crawl.

Swift tightened his grip on the oar. He'd have to do his best to get around the skiff; to deal with its rider.

A hand-to-hand struggle probably meant someone landing in the water with that shark, though.

Swift tried to give the *Strider* a push, but his arms were frozen.

All he could focus on was the weight of *The Star of Atlantis*, heavy with its map, in his pocket.

All this peril, all this distress, was upon him because of his obsession with the Star of Atlantis.

Swift's body seemed suddenly numb, the realization striking as paralysis, that this treasure chase might very well cost him his life.

At this moment, if he lost everything—his ship, his family, his life—in seeking a mythical pirate treasure, would the venture have been worth it? Was the Star of Atlantis worth dying for?

Swift had been in a life-or-death situation once before—with Ash, that terrible morning when Ash had tumbled off the dock and Swift had jumped into the rough waves after him.

Sometime later, he'd overheard Mum telling Caius that, hearing Swift shouting, she felt he was already lost.

To Mum, it was like Swift was calling for help from the beyond.

Swift had nearly died that day. And he would've died willingly for his friend.

But for this?

No.

No fabled treasure was worth dying for. And yet—he might die this dark morning, lost to its pursuit.

As slow, twilit moments slipped past, the impasse in the water between the *Star Strider* and the bleak skiff grew stale.

The sky shifted from sapphire to gunmetal gray. Dawn was coming.

But it made no difference.

A bank of sooty clouds was crowding the pale east. Clouds were roiling in from the north, too—maybe storm clouds.

There'd be no sun shafting into the cove to chase away thrashers and monsters and warm him. There'd be no *Regulus Borealis* advancing to his rescue.

The mist draping them felt as dead as a cold fish floating on acrid waves.

The dawning sky grew grim in the pass behind Grog Blossom, easing closer.

The thrasher in the depths assuredly rose.

Swift dragged his oar through the water, forcing the *Strider* to slip toward the skiff.

14

The roar of an engine split the stillness.

The skiff charged.

Swift—bloodless—lost his grip on the oar and slipped, landing square on his rump in the base of the *Strider*.

"Captain Corkscrew," growled a salty voice.

Swift jolted up. He knew that salty voice.

On the skiff's bench, a flashlight flaring on his whiskered grin, sat Justus.

Swift, quaking, gripping the mast, pulled himself to sitting. "Father?"

"Ay, me hearty!" Justus was roaring laughs. "It be your old da."

Swift flushed red-hot.

Justus was holding his belly, his face a puckish grin. "I be grateful to good old Peabrain, Jolly Stormcrow, and even Mister Hogwash for seeing ye to quiet waters."

Oh, god.

Swift sank deeper into the *Strider's* bowl. "Don't tell the others." He peeked over the *Strider's* gunwale. "Swear you won't tell."

Justus steered the skiff near. "Don't ye worry, Captain Corkscrew. Your secret's safe with Captain Justus."

He tied the *Strider* to his tow and reeled her close.

He gestured for Swift to step into the skiff.

Swift hesitated. He examined the deep gray water for the outline of the shark.

"Quite a beast that was," said Justus. "Come." He held out his hand. "The engine will have sent him cruising out to sea."

Swift took his father's hand and stepped across the gap.

Justus seated him on the skiff's bench and moved a duffle bag close.

Inside, a water bottle, snacks, and a blanket peeked out. "I don't suppose you brought provisions on your escapade?"

Swift reached for a water bottle.

The movement spurred the cramp in his shoulder.

Justus lifted a brow at Swift's pained face.

Swift contracted with the agony and doubled over.

Justus leveled his eyes with Swift's. "What, do you think, is the number one rule of sailing?"

Swift, hardly able to draw breath for the pain, couldn't speak.

Justus took the bottle from him and unscrewed it. "Come back alive."

Swift swallowed what he could of the water, then dropped to his knees in the base of the skiff, trying everything to ease the brutal cramp.

Justus caught his eye. "What would've happened if you'd tipped off the *Strider* in this state?"

"I couldn't swim," Swift managed.

"And?"

"I'd be drowned."

"So, what's the first rule of sailing?"

"Come back alive."

Justus rubbed Swift's shoulder and neck briskly.

It hurt like everything, but after a minute, the knot came loose, and Swift could move. He pulled onto the bench.

Behind Justus, the *Regulus* loomed through the pass.

Edric, Caius, and Trystan were there together, leaning their elbows on the rail.

The way they were watching him—Swift wished Justus had turned out to be Grog Blossom after all. Being done in by an undead pirate would be far better than what was about to happen.

"Out with it," said Justus. "What's on that mind?"

A sheet of mist blew in and swamped the *Regulus* from view.

Swift let his eyes find his father's. "They'll say that I'm nothing more than a lad. They'll tell me I'll never grow up."

Justus collected the oars. "Growing up isn't about running from storms. It's about weathering them. Sometimes, it's about conjuring them. And always, it's about coming back alive."

"I did weather a storm." Swift leaned forward, still trying to wrest his breath from the panic. "But they won't see it like that. They won't acknowledge that I sailed all on my own, all the way to this cove—swarming with sharks and who knows what else."

"That, you did. But you also tried to slip out from under us. To shortcut my instruction."

"I outsmarted the lot of you." Swift shouldn't have said it, but—there it was.

Justus raised his brow.

On the skiff, inside the sheet of shrouding mist dividing him from the gaze of his brothers, floating on his father's sea— his sea—Swift felt more leveled with Justus than he had before.

He sat up a bit straighter, took a deep breath, and let it out. "I outsmarted everyone. I launched the *Strider* while you all slept. Then I piloted her brilliantly. I took on a massive challenge, and I managed it. You didn't know at all what I was doing."

Justus held the oars out of the water. "Didn't I?"

The oars were marked: *Elias Byron.*

This skiff, then, belonged to Justus' long-time colleague— the psychiatrist, his close friend, Elias.

So—Justus had arranged for Elias to ready the skiff for him.

"If you'd seen me set off, you'd know I did everything right," said Swift. "She flew."

"I saw."

Swift settled back. "How long were you following me?"

"I kicked off the coast when you did. Though I was hidden by the mist, I was at the ready to snag you from the water, should the *Strider* have bucked you."

"So, you just let me take the *Strider*?"

Justus relaxed the oars. "You carry a powerful thirst for the sea—I know. It's been there practically all your life. And it's a thirst I recognize. I thought your mishap on the *Strider* this afternoon might've shaken your ambition, but your rigor with the sails today taught me better about your tenacity."

"And—you didn't force me back to shore." Could it be that Justus did understand him, even if only a bit?

Justus settled the motor to humming quietly in its lowest gear. "When I was your age, I had the same draw to the sea, toward accomplishment, that I sense in you. You're the fourth son I've raised up—a determined one, to be sure—and I'm a specialist in determined sons. I wagered you'd find your way out on the water by yourself one of these days. And then, yesterday, you got your hands on that old map. I judged it best that, if you were to have a go on the water alone, it'd better be on my watch."

"Why didn't you tell me all that back at home, then say we couldn't sail?"

"Free labor." Justus steadied the skiff back out through the mouth of the cove. "A stunt like this would land you swabbing the deck of the *Regulus* for the rest of the summer, doing the details with the housework, and helping me tend my paper mess of a study."

"Okay, but you're my father." Swift eyed him. "You could make me do all that anyway."

Justus glanced back at the *Regulus*, holding his three

grown sons. "You've not many summers left before you'll be as big as them. Do you ever think of that?"

Swift looked past his father at the dim faces of his brothers, looming through the mist.

Each was sketched with early morning stubble. Their arms, resting on the rail, were dense with muscles and shaded with hair.

A glance at his own self showed a hollow chest and skinny limbs, sinewy and peach fuzzed.

"No."

"Just a handful of years, and you'll be selecting a course in life. Whether you do the Practicum or not, you will be starting in with your University studies at sixteen. You've never wavered from that plan. And when that day—approaching so quickly—arrives, it won't be simply north and west you'll have to choose between. The world will stand before you, doors wide open."

Swift studied him sidelong.

"What are you getting at?"

Satisfaction spread across his father's face. "It's time we had our talk."

Swift froze on his bench, pinned like an insect.

He stared at the clever smile on his father as the realization settled that this adventure hadn't been at all by his own design.

Its engineer had been Justus.

His father's gaze on him was a heavy, steady pressure. Swift had always thought of Justus' fathering as a pressure to perform. But this seemed different than what he'd felt before.

He recognized it, now, as a pressure to become.

Justus leaned in.

"When the world stands before you, what will you do? You have academic and creative genius both at your disposal. Will you not seize that?"

The glinting red sun sheared a narrow band of gritty clouds in the south.

Its shine on the water was livening. It sparked in Swift a hunger to chase it.

"I feel born to be an adventurer. That's what I know."

"Adventure and treasure are well enough. But only to a point."

"No, think of it," said Swift. "Discovering ancient relics would be everything—wealth; pieces of history uncovered; mysteries solved. Granted, I went about it a little carelessly this morning, but if I really were to find the Star of Atlantis, Mum wouldn't have to work at all. And you could quit your job, too, and we could go sailing every day."

Justus studied him a moment. "I can't help but see something lingering beneath the surface of all that ambition."

"There's nothing lingering beneath the surface," said Swift. "I do know myself."

"Your fascination, your obsession, with sea venturing is—to some degree—about Ash."

"It's got nothing to do with him," said Swift. "I never think twice about him."

"Oh, I think it does," said Justus. "You perceive him to have what you think you lack."

"So? What if you're right? Haven't you and Mum always taught me to go after what I want."

"From a seasoned sailor to a novice one, I caution you not to waste your precious young years on the chasing of dreams. To quote one old sailor: '*Come hell. Come storm waters. Come the Kraken. I'll forsake all sound shores for the night-lighted passageways – untrodden reaches – for sun-brightened visions, for insights of stars.*'"

"That passage—how do you know it?"

"That passage is famous," said Justus. "Or, at least, it's well-known among those keen to seas and treasure, who've learned a bit of Celtic pirate lore."

Swift widened his eyes.

"I've told you, you're not the first Kingsley lad to catch wind of the Star of Atlantis."

"Then you must understand," said Swift. "Anyone, like

us, drawn to the sea, would forsake everything for a chance at exploring, at chasing down treasure. That passage says as much."

"The sailor who penned those words doesn't speak of old pirate relics, lad. He's after something richer. Higher."

"Untrodden reaches. Sun-brightened visions. Insights of stars," said Swift. "He's clearly speaking of adventure."

"He indeed craved adventure," said Justus. "And inspiration. Direction. A treasure for his heart to chase. You're a brilliant lad. Don't squander your giftedness dashing after trifles that won't last."

"The Star of Atlantis is no trifle." Swift focused on the glowing eastern sun, ascending through gray stripes of clouds. "It's widely thought to be real. And it's unfound. Imagine, if I were to discover it."

Justus watched the sun with Swift until it drifted into dawn-blue clouds, leaving the sea as dull as steel.

Justus looked Swift in the eye. "All right, let's imagine that. A bit of excitement, I suppose, finding the Star of Atlantis would bring. But what, then? Will you let your life be defined by a moment of boyhood triumph? Why not lay those hungry eyes of yours, not on the north, nor on skittish waves, nor on whispers of sunken treasure, but on an adventure where you could be a true hero?"

The tension in Swift's muscles eased some as he settled into listening.

"Wouldn't you like to learn how to heal pain?" Justus went on. "Isn't it better to address death straight on, rather than fear it? Would you not like to apply that brilliant mind of yours, those skilled hands, to an endeavor that might—as you desire—improve even the way medicine is practiced?"

That was exactly what he dreamed of accomplishing in medicine. But just because it was what he wanted—it didn't mean he was capable.

Swift lowered his gaze. "When we get back to your ship, if my brothers were to tease me about not being grown up, about lingering as a lad, they wouldn't be wrong."

"But you are growing up."

Swift's mind flashed through possible retorts until he settled on the one most likely to bore him a way out.

"I'm thirteen."

"And strikingly capable, you are, at thirteen," said Justus. "Your grades are higher than anyone in your school has ever achieved—including all your brothers. Your abilities with mathematics and chemistry are a decade beyond your years. Your skill with languages is simply savant. And you're a fair rival for each of your brothers, ambition-wise. Even as you sit here before me—at thirteen."

Swift imagined old Mister Hogwash, slumped behind Justus in the skiff, grinning.

How could Justus think it reasonable to pin him with the Talk just now, with all that pirate play bright in both their minds? With all Swift's commands still ringing in the fog, his mind still dazzling with the thought of the Star of Atlantis.

"The point I'd like to drive home is this," said Justus. "If you cast off your giftedness for the sake of chasing fables and dreams, I wager that you'll look back on the choices of your boyhood with regret. I'd like to see you embrace your giftedness, and the medical Practicum—entry-level training with a renowned doctor—is a perfect solution."

"Perhaps you could find me a renowned pirate to train with, instead."

Justus chuckled. Drew the oars. "Just think—you yourself would be capable of the feats Caius accomplishes every day in his rounds."

Despite Swift's doubts, after this day, managing sailing feats of which he'd not imagined himself capable—after sensing a close understanding from Justus—Swift felt himself soften more than he ever had at the thought.

"The Practicum accepts thirteen-year-old applicants," said Justus. "You'd apply now, then begin studying for your entrance exams just after your fourteenth birthday. Caius and I would, of course, help you prepare. And winning a seat, you'd no longer be just a passive observer of Caius in his stud-ies. My lad—you'd be his peer."

Swift loved every bit of the medicine Caius was studying.

But he couldn't help but be dizzied by Trystan's thou-sands of hours of cello practice.

By watching Caius leave to stay for days at the hospital, working as a tech of various kinds while his friends seemed to forget about him.

By hearing of how Edric's freedom had been vanquished in touring.

Their workloads would seem nothing to what Swift, competing for the Practicum, would face.

"I can't handle gore like you and Caius can," Swift tried.

"Handling medicine's grotesqueness comes with practice."

Justus might be right that a stronger stomach might come. But the suffering. Doctors must stand by and watch suffering.

"But"—Swift looked his father in the eyes—"the fox."

Swift's stomach still ached from the sight of its torn leg, mangled from a trap or a fight. His ears still seemed to ring with the animal's whining.

He'd tried every way to approach the fox, to gain his trust so he could get him to a vet. But every time he moved near, a rumbling growl would replace the whine. The fox was near death and probably knew it. And all that pain and terror kept the poor thing from peace.

"Doctors deal in suffering, to be sure," said Justus.

"Not just suffering," said Swift. "Doctors must deal in death."

"Their business, though, is the easing of fear and of pain. Think on the stories that Caius comes home with. And think of how gentle he is with your own bumps and bruises."

Caius on the ship, his face now plain through the thinning mist, was smiling. His eyes were trained hard on Swift.

He seemed to know the Justus Talk was happening.

Caius was quite happy with the current their father had pushed him into. But Caius was Caius.

Swift laid his gaze back on his father. "What if I'm nothing more than a lad? What if that's all I'll ever be?"

"Being a lad is well enough. But keep in mind—you will be a man, and much longer than you'll be a lad. Part of being a lad is planning to be a man."

"But that's just it." Swift cast a glance at his brothers. "You expect me to be like them—I couldn't possibly be."

Justus, too, fixed his gaze on the *Regulus*. "Do you know why I named my ship as I did?"

The *Regulus Borealis*—the King of the North Wind.

"I imagine it's because you're something like Odin," said Swift. "Kingly and powerful."

"I don't have to tell you that 'Regulus' not only means 'king,' but it's also the name of a star."

Regulus was a star. One of Swift's favorite stars. Regulus was visible at this moment, coasting to night's end in the west.

Swift pointed to where it was falling behind the gray veil of mist. "It's that star—Alpha Regulus. Leo's brightest star. 'The Heart of the Lion.' It's fitting for you."

"Regulus is no single star—but a star system," said Justus. "Regulus is made up of four stars, all told."

Swift lowered his eyes from the dusky west and rested them instead on his father.

"Four stars, very powerful, each in their own way," said Justus. "Four stars who may influence one another and who may clash from time to time."

"Are you sure there are four stars in that system?" asked Swift. "Not three?"

"Four stars," said Justus.

Swift and his father together watched Regulus, the lion's heart, vanish into the water of dawn.

At its disappearance, Justus coasted the skiff on toward his ship.

Swift readied the ropes to lash the skiff to the brigantine. "Are you giving me a choice in this, or will you force me in?"

"This will be your choice." Justus guided the skiff's last

approach, to the ship's starboard side. "But I wager—I know what you'll choose."

The way Justus managed his balance, how he eyed the ship and precisely laid his course—how skillfully he executed it—charmed Swift.

"When did you start sailing?" Swift asked him.

"When I was about your age." Justus hauled over the *Strider*, bobbing in the water behind the skiff. "Like you, I was more suited to the sea than most. And I had a chase or two myself—once even after the Star of Atlantis."

"If you actually went after it, then you must not think it's wholly a fool's chase."

Justus half-smiled. "I'll concede that part of being a man is remembering to still be a lad."

Swift sat back, studying Justus' pale eyes—silver in the steely dawn. "Then, we understand one another."

"I'd say so."

"Does that mean I can skip the grounding?"

Justus chuckled. "On the first cool day of autumn, we'll talk about parole."

Swift gazed up the hull of the *Regulus*, holding his three waiting brothers, their courses all laid by their father's aspirations.

Justus glanced again at Swift. "Would you say that we have a heading?"

On the sea, in all this mist, his spine still tingly with the chase, his heart still agitated by the thought of the thrasher's needled mouth, his eyes still dazzled by the flickering blue light in the water, old Mister Hogwash leering in his imagination—Swift found himself incapable of picturing any part of his future.

The only pull he felt was stirred by the sea heaving over the very old Earth; the faint silver stars blinking out.

"On the first cool day of autumn," said Swift, "we'll talk about your plan."

Justus raised his brow. "Be assured that you and I shall speak again."

Swift stood beside his father, and they together tied lines, fixing fast the skiff and the dinghy to hooks on the brigantine's hull.

They climbed the netting up the ship's flank and crossed the rail.

Caius took the blanket Swift was gripping and draped him with a dry one. "Nice bandana."

Not meeting his eyes, Swift took it off and gave it to him.

"That was some crafty sailing, little brother," said Trystan, handing him a water bottle.

Swift, glancing at Trystan, took the bottle. The smile on him didn't look like teasing.

Caius guided Swift to the bench and made him sit.

Edric stood aside, arms crossed.

If maturity and reserve were what he expected, he had to be disgusted with Swift, after what he'd seen.

Swift winced, waiting for Edric to lay in.

Edric approached. "You want a word of advice, Little Brother?"

Swift pulled his knees into his chest.

"Do I have a choice?"

"If you want to go for that Practicum, do it," said Edric. "But whatever you choose, remember what you felt this night, driven wholly by your own heart."

Swift, staring at Edric, let down one leg, then the other.

"If I didn't know better," said Caius, "I'd say you were proud of him."

"I am proud of the lad," said Edric. "Maybe he's more like me than you. Maybe he's bold enough to dare his own way."

"I thought you wanted me grown up," said Swift.

"That's exactly what I want," said Edric. "But growing up isn't about falling into line. It's about finding your own way."

The tension loosened in Swift's back, letting him sit all the way up. "I thought you'd say you wanted father to skin me."

"I'll give you that what you pulled was risky and stupid."

Edric smiled the merest bit. "But it's exactly the sort of risky and stupid, at thirteen, I would've tried."

Edric reached to scruff Swift's curls, soaked with mist.

This time, Swift didn't feel the impulse to dodge.

Edric moved Swift's hair out of his eyes, slicking it back, to one side, the way he wore his. "Only, I would've gotten away with it."

Caius snuck Swift a half-smile and a fist to bump.

"Well, then." Trystan turned toward Justus. "Will we be heading home?"

Justus went to the steering deck. "Swift has found a treasure map." He laid his gaze on the north. "I judge it best that we set out to discover whether it's legitimate"—he glanced at Swift—"or Hogwash."

The End

DEDICATION

*To my colleagues in Higher Education and Adult Education
who unceasingly support and encourage my writing ambitions.
Thank you for being kind enough to let me talk about writing
as much as I want over dinner.
You keep me sailing in strong winds.*

*Thanks to my writing community, to Tim Storm—ever a strong
support and a needle pointing north.
And to my insightful critique partners—thanks for presenting
me with the opportunity to grow before you as a writer,
week by week by week.*

*Thank you to Andy Chamberlain for your insightful teaching
and guidance, for lending Swift your voice, and for introducing
me to Devon Cream Tea.*

*To Tara Lewis and Denis Caron, you have my endless
gratitude for showing me the ropes of publishing. Your interest
in this series and your encouragement to me as a writer have
helped me believe that I really can do this.*

*And especially – thank you to my friends and fellow adult
education leaders. Kim Kunce, Matt Beasland, and our
IACEA colleagues, whose kindness and enthusiasm to read a
sequel to **Where Fish Can Breathe** inspired the creation of
The Strider and the Regulus.*

READ THE STAR OF ATLANTIS SERIES!

*The Strider and the Regulus, The Star of Atlantis
& The Shepherd of the Stars*

A starry-eyed boy.
A cryptic map. A mythical treasure.
What perils await in the chasing of dreams?

"*Wagner has a beautiful and poetic writing style which serves to enhance the descriptive detail she provides to her novels. This gives her books a whimsical and otherworldly quality that supports the fantastical elements within them. Readers who appreciate thoughtful narratives that focus on the human condition within the context of charming and memorable stories will quickly fall for this series and its immersive quality.*
"*The medical and scientific elements found within this book help readers puzzle out the question of what is true in Swift's world alongside the legend and lore. This is a satisfying series that will speak to young adult readers and adults alike.*"
- Mary R. Lanni, MLIS, *Reedsy Discovery*

ALSO BY TRICIA D. WAGNER

WHAT MANNER OF LEGENDS MIGHT DARKNESS CONCEAL?

"SUN CHILD OF THE MOOR IS A WELL-WRITTEN, BEAUTIFULLY POETIC, FANTASTICAL TALE, EXPERTLY BLENDING MAGIC WITH REALITY. SYLPHIC FOLKLORE IS UNIQUE TO THIS BOOK AND HOLDS THE POWER OF BELIEVABILITY THANKS TO WAGNER'S MASTERFUL WRITING. THE FAMILIAL INTERACTIONS ARE REMINISCENT OF A WRINKLE IN TIME, MAKING IT A DELIGHTFULLY IMMERSIVE TALE OF LOVE AND PERSONAL GROWTH, WELL SUITED TO YOUNG AND ADULT READERS WHO ENJOY EXPLORING THE WORLD'S UNLIMITED POSSIBILITIES THROUGH A MAGICAL LENS."
-MARY R. LANNI, MLIS, *REEDSY DISCOVERY*

"SUN CHILD OF THE MOOR, WITH ITS LIVELY, ENGAGING ACTION WILL ENCOURAGE DISCUSSION AND DEBATE IN READER CIRCLES ABOUT THE CONSEQUENCES OF SPECIAL ABILITIES AND THE CONTRAST BETWEEN IMAGINATION AND REALITY, MAKING THIS BOOK A TOP RECOMMENDATION ABOVE MANY OTHER ACTION-PACKED FANTASIES."
-D. DONOVAN, SR. REVIEWER, *MIDWEST BOOK REVIEW*

FREE EBOOK

NIGHT SWIFTLY FALLING
BY TRICIA D. WAGNER

EIGHT-YEAR-OLD SWIFT IS LOST IN DREAMS OF SEA
LEGENDS AND PIRATE ADVENTURES, UNTIL AN
ENCOUNTER WITH THE DEADLY POWER OF THE
OCEAN SHOCKS HIM INTO REALITY.
SWIFT STRUGGLES TO HANG ONTO HIS CHILDHOOD
FANTASIES, BUT HIS NEW UNDERSTANDING OF THE
FRAGILE NATURE OF LIFE AND FRIENDSHIPS
THREATENS TO SWAMP HIS HOPE.
UNDER THE GUIDANCE OF HIS OLDER BROTHER,
CAIUS, SWIFT MUST LEARN TO BRAVE THE CHAL-
LENGING WAVES OF CHANGE WITHOUT LOSING
HIMSELF TO THEIR DESTRUCTION.

TO GET YOUR FREE EBOOK, VISIT -
NIGHT SWIFTLY FALLING

ABOUT THE AUTHOR

TRICIA D. WAGNER IS AN AWARD-WINNING NOVELIST, POET, AND SHORT STORY WRITER. SHE GREW UP IN AMARILLO, TEXAS, CHASING STORMS, RIDING STALLIONS, SOJOURNING THROUGH PAINTED CANYONS, DISAPPEARING INTO FLOATING MESAS UNDER STARRY SKIES.

SHE NOW LIVES IN ROCKFORD, ILLINOIS (THOUGH THE TRUTH IS, SHE'S A CITIZEN OF A DOZEN FICTIONAL COUNTRIES). TRICIA WORKS IN RESEARCH AND LIVES DAY TO DAY WONDERSTRUCK BUT LUCKILY CAN FEEL HER WAY ABOUT THIS TERRIFYING, BEAUTIFUL EARTH THROUGH WRITING.

TRICIA HAS PIECES PUBLISHED IN THE *WRITE CITY MAGAZINE*, *CHICAGO NEWA*, *WORD OF ART 3D*, *LITERARY YARD*, AND *MIDWEST REVIEW*.

TO LEARN MORE ABOUT TRICIA, SIGN UP FOR HER READERS' CLUB, AND HEAR ABOUT UPCOMING RELEASES, VISIT:

WWW.TRICIAWAGNER.COM

AUTHOR'S NOTE

I love connecting with readers and writers. If, you're interested in stories, then you're a kindred spirit to me, and I have lots more in store for you. To quote another kindred spirit in writing, Jedi Master Stephen King:

"Writing is magic, as much as the water of life as any other art. The water is free. So drink. Drink and be filled up."

If you're interested not only in stories, but in story creation, visit my website and sign up to receive a FREE 'Story Kickoff Character Worksheet.'

I designed this tool for that first moment of getting our feet wet at the brink of a story.

To get your free worksheet, visit:
www.TriciaWagner.com